AIK

Aiken, Joan

Up the chimney
down and other
stories

UP
THE
CHIMNEY
DOWN

A CHARLOTTE ZOLOTOW BOOK
CZ

UP THE CHIMNEY DOWN

and other stories

JOAN AIKEN

HARPER & ROW, PUBLISHERS

Up the Chimney Down
and Other Stories
Text copyright © 1984 by Joan Aiken Enterprises Ltd

"The Gift-Giving" first appeared in the United States in an
anthology entitled Sixteen, published by Delacorte for the
State of Connecticut, edited by Donald Gallo.

Designed by Joyce Hopkins
1 2 3 4 5 6 7 8 9 10
First American Edition

Library of Congress Cataloging in Publication Data
Aiken, Joan, 1924–
Up the chimney down and other stories.

"A Charlotte Zolotow book."
Contents: The last chimney cuckoo — Miss Hooting's
legacy — The gift-giving — [etc.]
1. Short stories, English. [1. Short stories]
I. Title
PZ7.A2695Up 1985   [Fic]   85-42642
ISBN 0-06-020036-7
ISBN 0-06-020037-5 (lib. bdg.)

To Treva and Jeremy Wurmfeld

Contents

The Last
Chimney Cuckoo

In the village of Musselboys, which is in Essex, they sing
a skipping rhyme that goes:

> Chimney cuckoo, come today
> Lay your egg in my chimney!
> Cheese and butter I will pay,
> A silver spoon, a load of hay,
> Gold by the bag, wine by the keg,
> All for a chimney cuckoo's egg!

They sing the song in Musselboys because that village
happens to lie on the straight line taken by the chimney
cuckoos on their spring flight northward across England
from Folkestone to Cape Wrath. The line also includes
Brentwood, Huntingdon, Newark, Knaresborough, Jed-
burgh, Abernethy, and Inverness. When they leave the
coast of Scotland the chimney cuckoos go on to the Faroes
and Iceland.

Or did. There are very, very few chimney cuckoos left now.

Anna Fern the ballet dancer discovered this fact after she bought a lion from her Uncle Fred.

Why did she buy the lion? At the time when she did so, Anna was mad keen to have the lion, whose name was Ulysses. And Fred, whose name was Fred Lassitude, was equally anxious to be rid of it. He had no use for a lion. He had been a butler, in the service of Lord George Gilsland the famous explorer; and Fred's ambition, when Lord George died, was to own a nice pub, one with a big garden, perhaps by the river in Putney. He had been hoping for a tidy bit of money in Lord George's will. Imagine his annoyance when he found that all he had inherited was a lion—and a fussy, vegetarian lion at that— one that would eat only rice pudding and corn bread and porridge and fruitcake and bran flakes. And wanted a whole lot of those things, what's more, as much in one day as would feed a whole pack of starving hyenas.

And not only that, but, according to the lawyer who came to explain the terms of Lord George's will, the lion had some sort of curse attached to it.

"You were with Lord George, I believe, when he ac- quired the lion?" inquired Mr. Feltpoint the lawyer, handing Fred Lassitude a slip of paper to sign. It said: "Received: one live lion, Nemean species, male, five years old, in good health, responds to name Ulysses."

"Certainly I was," snapped the butler, dashing the sig- nature Fred Lassitude angrily across the receipt and pass-

2

ing it back to the lawyer. "Went with him everywhere
he traveled for the last twenty-five years. Crumpets in the
tropics, I served him; toast at the North Pole, *with* the
crusts cut off; never a word of complaint."

And what's it got me for my trouble? A perishing lion,
he thought.

"We'd been shipwrecked," he went on peevishly. "Adrift
in the Pacific, in a dinghy. Not a ship in sight for days.
Down to our last Bath Oliver biscuit. And then we spot
this raft drifting toward us. Hopeful we were, at first. But
then we see what's on it. Nothing but a white lion cub.
Dead to the world, it looked; limp and draggled, skin and
bone. 'Still, maybe there'd be a mouthful of meat on
him,' I says, and Lord George, *he* says, 'Certainly not,
Lassitude, the idea! That there, I'd have you know, is a
Nemean lion cub, a rare, endangered species. I wouldn't
eat that cub if it was our last chance of life, Lassitude.
There's plenty of us humans, too many,' he says, 'but
you could look all over Asia and Africa and I doubt if
you'd find half a dozen Nemean lions left.' And with that
he hauls it on board and feeds it our last Bath Oliver,
what we'd been saving, softened up with a bit of dew
we'd collected in the compass case."

Lassitude looked annoyed all over again at the memory.
He was a thin sallow prim gray-haired flat-faced soft-
spoken man with a small mouth like a hyphen.

"I reckoned we were done for," he went on, "but, half
an hour later, along comes one of those native war canoes
with a bunch of Mytholesian savages on board, who pick

3

us up and take us to land. 'Ulysses has brought us luck, Lassitude,' says Lord George. *I* thought the natives meant to eat us, but it's true that when they noticed the lion cub, who was just beginning to stir and open his eyes and give a lick or two at Lord George's hand—then they couldn't do enough for us. Took us along to the Pharmacy—that's the name of their witch doctor's palace. There was so many elephants' tusks and bird-of-paradise feathers dangling on the old fellow that he looked like a walking Christmas tree. Stared hard at us, he did, stared at the lion cub, bowed so low half his tusks fell off, and arranged for us to be taken over the mountains to a trading station."

"And he told Lord George about the curse, I suppose?"

"How should *I* know?" Lassitude answered irritably. "They was jabbering away an hour together in Polygonese. *I* could never be fished to get my tongue around those native lingoes. The nogs can understand plain English well enough when they choose to, if you speak loud and slow. Curse? How should I know? Anything about a curse was all between old Mumbo-Jumbo and Lord George. Myself, I don't believe in it."

"The curse states (I have it here in an Appendix to the Will) that any person making money by selling the lion will suffer a Misfortune within two days. And any other person who is a party to the sale will suffer a similar but lesser Misfortune. Possibly that is why Lord George himself never attempted to dispose of the animal?"

"Oh, no, sir." Lassitude sniffed. "Barmy about the

beast, he was. Called it Fido. Traveled all over, looking for another one, a companion for it. Took it with him. Might I inquire, sir," he went on, and now there was a definite note of grievance in his tone, "might I ask who got the rest of Lord George's property?"

The lawyer rose to his feet, glancing through the window, as he did so, at Ulysses the lion, who was roaming restlessly about the small London garden. Ulysses measured nine feet from nose to tail tassel; he was snowy white all over and had eyes like rose diamonds.

"All Lord George's other possessions are to be sold," replied Mr. Feltpoint, "and the money from the sale, and the royalties from his travel books, will go to establish a fund for the preservation of endangered species. The Nemean lion and the chimney cuckoo are specifically mentioned. Thank you, Mr. Lassitude. Good day to you."

"Chimney cuckoos, indeed," muttered Lassitude, seeing the lawyer out. But he muttered the words under his breath. "Chimney cuckoos, indeed. Who gives a burnt toast crust for *chimney cuckoos?*"

Two days later, curse or no curse, Fred Lassitude sold the Nemean lion for a substantial sum to his niece Anna Fern. If the sale's only in the family, he thought, it very likely don't count like a regular shop sale. And we won't let the news get about. Anna's a sensible girl. Quiet. Not one to blab.

Anna Fern, his sister's daughter, was a ballet dancer. Single-minded, ambitious, her mind set on nothing but her dancing, she had gone straight to the top, and could easily afford a Nemean lion. She had just been paid very well for dancing in a film called *Jungle Minuet*, and she fancied the idea of keeping a lion in her garden. The first minute she set eyes on Ulysses, she longed to possess him. She paid her uncle by check and phoned a friend with a truck, the kind that theatrical sets are moved in, to pick up Ulysses and take him to where Anna lived in North Kensington.

"It's no use expecting him to touch meat or fish," Lassitude warned her. "For he'll eat nothing but blessed rice pudding and Christmas cake and rolled oats and French toast. And plenty of that! He'll drink apple juice, but milk is what he likes best."

"Oh, yes, of course, very well," Anna replied inattentively. She disliked her uncle and wished to get out of his company as fast as possible; also she was dying to show off her new belonging to her friends. She hardly paid any attention as Fred told her about the curse.

"I don't suppose it really works, do you?" she interrupted. "Anyway, as you say, inside the family it probably doesn't count." And she jumped into a cab and ordered it to follow the truck.

Lassitude retired indoors, rubbing his hands, to lay plans for his pub. I could call it The White Lion, he thought. Like his lordship said, the beast did bring me luck.

Two days later Fred Lassitude had the misfortune to be run over by a bus and killed, while his niece Anna suffered the minor, but still very inconvenient, mishap of slipping on a cake of soap in the bath and breaking her leg. She had to wear an enormous white plaster cast from hip to ankle, and was told that she would not be able to dance for six months.

Anna was aghast at this setback. Not dance for *six months*? How could she bear it? All her friends and rivals would be getting the best parts, while she could do nothing but sit in her basement flat with her enormous white motionless leg up on a sofa and look out of her window at Ulysses pacing hurriedly around her tiny garden (which was about the size of a bathroom) as if he were mad with boredom. To and fro, he went, up and down, back and forth, swishing his long tail with the tassel on it. Pad, pad. Swish, swish. Around and around. Up and down. Anna shoved up the sash window, put her head out, and called, "Can't you sit *still* for a minute?" The lion took no notice of her. But about ten minutes later he reared up his head and roared—a long, hungry, forsaken, solitary, heartbroken sound. Perhaps he misses Lord George, Anna thought uncomfortably. But she had too many troubles of her own to bother about those of a lion. He'll just have to get used to it, she thought. And, after all her friends had come to visit her, and sympathize about her leg, and admire Ulysses out there in the garden, she decided that it would be sensible to go off to Bermuda for a couple of months. In Bermuda, at least, she would be able to lie in the sun.

To pay the fare she half considered selling Ulysses— after all, what use was he, really?—but then decided that it might be wiser not to. Better safe than sorry. I could rent him out, though, she thought; and did so, to someone she knew who was about to make a film about St. Jerome. The rental money would pay for the trip to Bermuda; and when she came back she would think of something to do with Ulysses, maybe give him to the zoo in exchange for free visits—Anna liked going to the zoo—or, very likely she could earn a tidy sum by hiring him out to advertising companies. Meanwhile she arranged for a neighbor to feed him.

In spite of lying in the sun, Anna found that her leg didn't heal in Bermuda as fast as it ought. When she came home, without the plaster, she still had quite a bad limp. Dancing was out of the question.

When she first saw Ulysses, she was both annoyed and upset. In her absence he had grown shockingly thin. His ribs showed like the bars of a cage. And his beautiful thick white coat had grown lank, staring, patchy—great hanks had fallen out—no advertising agency would look at him while he was in such a state! His tail dragged on the ground, as if he could no longer be bothered to swish it about. He limped, almost as badly as Anna herself. Only his eyes still burned with a feverish fire. And the neighbors complained bitterly, because at about five every morning—every blessed day, they said—he howled, hungrily, hollowly, harrowingly—every single day he woke them up, the neighbors said, and then they couldn't get back to sleep, but had to lie awake thinking about all

8

their problems. Would Anna please make arrangements to keep him somewhere else, they said.

Anna was greatly put out by all this. She had spent more than she ought on the trip to Bermuda, Ulysses cost a lot in rice pudding and fruitcake, she was no longer able to dance, so could not earn money—and the lion was driving her mad with his misery.

"What's the matter with you? Can't you tell me?" she said to him, but he only roared heartbrokenly. His appetite was growing smaller and smaller; only one fruitcake a day, only two bowls of rice pudding. Anna kept nibbling the uneaten cakes that stood in the larder, so while he grew thinner, she grew fatter. Suppose he should die, she worried. Another curse might come into play then; she hated to think what might happen. Perhaps it would be better to sell him? Selling a Nemean lion is probably not so bad as allowing one to starve himself to death.

For the first time Anna began to think seriously about her lion.

When she had done this for about a week, she telephoned her Cousin Bert.

Bert Fern had no phone of his own. He lived on a barge that wandered all over England, along the canals. In order to get in touch with Bert you had to call the combined pub and post office at the village of Tiny Dunmow. They would take a message. And when Bert's boat, the *Queen Anne's Lace*, next came nosing along the canal and tied up at the pub, Bert would receive the message. Sometimes it took a week, sometimes three months.

Anna was lucky. In a fortnight Bert phoned his cousin.

"Hello there, Annie. What's the matter?" Bert knew that Anna would only phone him when she wanted something. "Fed up with dancing, are you?" he said. "I knew you would be, sooner or later."

"No, it's not that at all," she snapped. "My leg's busted— I *can't* dance. No, I've got this lion I want your advice about."

"A lion, eh?" said Bert, interested. "Can you bring him down here?"

"Of course not! With my bad leg I can't drive. You come here."

Bert hated London, but Anna didn't care about that.

"Well, all right," said he. "Matter of fact, I want some information from the Natural History Museum about chimney cuckoos."

So next day Bert came to call on Anna. The cousins were very different. Fern was a good surname for Bert: with his brownish, reddish bush of hair and beard, his twinkling brown eyes, brown skin, and his raggedy worn old tweed jacket, which he never bothered to replace though there were threads hanging down from it all over— he looked like a bracken bank in autumn. He left the dangling threads because he said birds sometimes used them for nest building.

"So, what's all this about a lion, then, Annie?" he asked as he came through the door. Then he looked past her into the garden and saw Ulysses, and said, "Lorda-mercy! You certainly got a problem on your hands there! But what a stunner! What a right 'un! Here then, Beauty," he said, going past Anna into the garden, and in a moment he was patting and scratching Ulysses, rubbing him under the chin, pulling his ears and rumpling his mane as if they'd gone to kindergarten together.

"But what's the matter with him, Bert?" asked Anna when he came in again, with Ulysses looking after him sadly.

"Why, it's plain, ain't it? Use your nut! Didn't old whatsisname—Lord George—travel all over taking Ulysses wherever he went?"

"Yes, I believe so," said Anna. "Uncle Fred did say something about that."

"Well, then! He was looking for another Nemean lion, a friend for Ulysses. But he never found one. I've heard tell there's none left in the world. If you were Ulysses, wouldn't that make *you* sad?"

"Well, I don't know," said Anna, trying to think about it. "That would make you sort of special, wouldn't it?"

"Oh, you're just a silly girl," said Bert. "*I* wouldn't fancy it. No more than I'd want to be a chimney cuckoo."

"Chimney cuckoo? What's that got to do with Ulysses?"

"Why, they're a species of white cuckoo. Getting very rare. Instead of laying eggs in other birds' nests, like regular cuckoos, they lay their eggs down chimneys. At five o'clock in the morning."

"Why at that time?" said Anna, yawning a little.

11

"Use your loaf, Annie! You lay an egg down a chimney during daytime, the fire'll be lit, won't it? So the egg would roast. But at five o'clock there's just a nice pile of warm ash in the hearth, exactly right for hatching, and soft, so's the egg won't break."

"But suppose someone comes and lights the fire, or shovels out all the ash? Wouldn't the egg get broken?"

"Yeah. Nine times out of ten. That's why there are so few chimney cuckoos left." Bert sighed deeply. "'Tis a beautiful egg, too—big and gray, about as big as a pigeon's egg, with a few silvery spots. The kids in Mussel-boys, where my barge is now, they have a rhyme:

Chimney cuckoo, what shall I do?
Put the egg inside your shoe
Dance a jig in your cotton socks
Dance on top of a pillar-box;
Balance up there on one leg
Catch the chimney cuckoo's egg
In your shoe, higher and higher,
Seven times for your heart's desire!

That's another reason why chimney cuckoos are scarce," Bert said. "If kids find the eggs they try to throw and catch them seven times. And the eggs mostly get broken."

"How stupid," said Anna, yawning again. "But never mind about cuckoos—tell me what I can do about Ulysses. Isn't there some tonic I could give him so he'd get his looks back?"

"Best thing," said Bert, "would be for you to travel

with him, looking for another Nemean lion."

"How could I afford to do that? Besides, I haven't the time. He must manage without."

"I reckon I can't help you, then," said Bert. And he shrugged and left her. But he gazed sadly, regretfully back at Ulysses, who was now slouching around the tiny garden with his head hanging low, too dejected even to look after the man who had been kind to him.

Pity Annie wouldn't think to give the feller to me, Bert thought. Traveling the canals on the *Queen Anne's Lace* might cheer the beggar up.

Bert went back to his boat. But, after he had gone, Anna recalled what he had said about chimney cuckoos.

If I could get hold of a chimney cuckoo's egg, she thought, I'd be able to throw and catch it seven times, I'm sure.

She was right there, for dancers are clever at throwing and catching. And Anna could balance better, even with her stiff leg, than most people can with two good legs.

I know what I'll do, Anna thought.

Full of excitement and purpose, she sent an advertisement to *The Times* to be printed every day for a week: *Anna Fern needs a Chimney Cuckoo's Egg.*

The month was April, it was a good time to advertise; cuckoos were about.

A man called Mick Muddigust, who ran a TV news program, happened to see Anna's advertisement. He had known her when she was at ballet school, and he invited her to come and talk on his television program about why she wanted the egg. Anna reckoned this would be a useful way of getting her wish more widely known, and she would get paid too.

"Why do you want a chimney cuckoo's egg, Anna?" Mick Muddigust asked on his program. "That seems a queer thing to want."

"Oh, no, Mick, not at all," said Anna. "Not everyone knows this, but if you can toss and catch a chimney cuckoo's egg in your shoe seven times, standing on one leg on a pillar-box, you will get your heart's desire. You have to do it without breaking the egg, of course."

"Is that so?" said Mick Muddigust. "And what's your heart's desire, eh, Anna? To be the best dancer in the world, I suppose? Well, folks, now's your chance to help Anna," he said, turning to address the television viewers all over the country. "Find a chimney cuckoo's egg in your fireplace, and give her her heart's desire. Or give yourself your own heart's desire—just toss and catch the egg in your shoe seven times, standing on one leg on a pillar-box. And if you can do that without breaking the egg, then send it to Anna."

Well, if that didn't start a wild craze!

All up and down the track of the chimney cuckoos' path of flight, people were hunting in their fireplaces for eggs. Just here and there one was to be found, and then, my word, the excitement. Big money was offered— twenty, fifty, a hundred, five hundred pounds. Eggs were auctioned. Folk made mad bids. Eggs were faked and forged—people painted pigeons' eggs gray with silver spots.

Questions were asked in Parliament. Professors wrote in to the Natural History Museum, asking was it all right to hard boil the egg before throwing and catching it. For, so far, among those who had found eggs and tried the trick, no one had managed to throw and catch the egg as many as seven times. One boy got as far as six. But then he dropped the egg. Most folk dropped the egg by the second or third throw.

Bert Fern, traveling to and fro, up and down the country in the *Queen Anne's Lace,* didn't have a TV set, so he missed seeing his cousin make her appearance and her request; but he heard tell of it soon enough, for the talk wherever he went was about chimney cuckoos' eggs. When he found out the reason why, it made Bert so angry, though he was a mild-natured fellow, that he went to a public telephone and phoned his Cousin Anna.

"How *dare* you do such a thing? Do you know how many eggs have been smashed, because of your silly appeal? Thousands! Thousands of cuckoos will never hatch, all because of you."

Anna flew into a rage. "I did it for that dratted lion! I wish I'd never bought him. I was going to wish for a mate for him."

"A likely tale!" said Bert.

"Excuse me!" she snapped furiously. "There's someone at the door. I can't talk just now." And she thumped down the receiver.

The person at the door proved to be a messenger from Rokeby's, the auctioneers, with a notice informing Anna that they had received two chimney cuckoos' eggs and would be disposing of these at their salesroom the next morning at ten-thirty A.M.

Anna went along to the salesroom the next day, of course, but without much hope. Her savings were nearly gone, and she didn't see how she could possibly manage to buy one of the eggs.

Sure enough, the bidding for the first egg soon went up into thousands of pounds. The owner of a hundred oil wells was there bidding—he said he had managed to buy everything in the world except a chimney cuckoo's egg, and he was bound to have it. Sure enough, at thirty thousand pounds everyone else dropped out, and he bought it for thirty thousand pounds, one penny. He had been drinking champagne mixed with strawberry juice right through the sale, and when the egg was sold to him he let out a wild yippee.

Then he called for a pillar-box. One was wheeled in on a dolly and hoisted up onto the auctioneer's platform.

"Now!" bawled the oil-well owner. "Now I'm going to show all you folks how to set about getting your—hic!—heart's desire. Hic! Just you hold that egg while I get my boots off," he said to the auctioneer. "Mind you don't drop it. Right! Now don't anybody hold me back, for I'm agoing to dance a Polish mazurka on top of that there pillar-box!"

And with one spring he bounded in his sock feet onto the top of the pillar-box and jumped up and down on it. Everybody laughed and clapped. Then he asked the auctioneer to pass him the egg, and he put it into one of his cowboy boots and began tossing it up in the air. Once he tossed it—twice—then the egg broke and his hopes were over. Not only that, but he suffered some kind of paralytic fit, fell to the ground, and had to be carried away on a stretcher. He was not a young man.

Everybody was a bit glum and quiet while the second egg was sold off. Anna knew now that she hadn't a hope, so wasn't paying much attention. She just noticed that the second egg went for less—only eighteen thousand pounds and nine pence to a person she couldn't see, a quiet-voiced man.

After the sale was over, though, somebody tapped her on the shoulder, and said, "This egg is for you, miss."

"Egg, what egg?" says Anna, suddenly shivering.

"Why, this egg that I have just purchased," says a smallish, baldish man in a fur coat. "My brother and I, miss, have always been great admirers of your dancing, and I—we—would wish you to accept this egg as a token of our esteem, and I—we—hope it makes you the greatest dancer in the whole world, for we were greatly saddened to hear about your accident," he says.

Well, wasn't Anna amazed and excited then! When she had thanked the small man, and thanked him again— "Won't you give us an exhibition of your skill, miss?" he says, and without more ado Anna took off her shoes. She always did wear little soft ballet slippers, so that was what she had worn to the sale.

With a little skip she hopped up on top of the pillar-box, which was still on the auctioneer's platform, and everybody clapped and cheered. Then, standing on her good leg, Anna tossed and caught the chimney cuckoo's egg in her ballet slipper. One—two—three—four—five—six—seven times. And, my word, didn't everybody clap and cheer then!

"Quick now, tell me what's your heart's desire, Miss Fern," said a newspaperman from the *Daily Hurrah*, who was there to report on the sale. And—whether by chance or from excitement, or because she forgot, or because it was the truth—Anna never gave poor Ulysses a single thought, but said, "I wish to become the best dancer in the whole world!"

And then, as she jumped down from the pillar-box, the chimney cuckoo's egg fell from her hand—fell and was smashed.

Some time went by, after that. Anna was too busy to give a lot of thought to her Cousin Bert. Maybe thinking of him made her uncomfortable, so she didn't choose to.

She was asked to dance, of course, in Paris, Rome, San Francisco, Tokyo, Moscow, Peking. She never stopped traveling. Everybody wanted to see her dance. The bouquets that she was sent would have filled the whole of Ireland, if they had been laid side by side. The money she was paid would have bought half a dozen islands with palaces on them. But she would never have had time to live in them.

That was how it went at the start. Luckily, after a while,

she had the sense, now she was so busy dancing here, there, and everywhere, to send the lion, Ulysses, to her Cousin Bert. She didn't sell Ulysses, she gave him, not wishing to risk any more misfortunes. Anyway, she knew that Bert had no money. "Ulysses will be better with you," she wrote. "Maybe traveling on the canals will keep him hopeful." She did not hear how Ulysses liked it on the *Queen Anne's Lace*, for Bert never wrote back.

Chimney cuckoos were extinct, the newspapers said, due to the foolish craze that had started up. The craze died down again fairly soon; but that was mainly because there were no more eggs to be found.

As the years floated by, Anna went on dancing. Everybody agreed that she was the best dancer in the world. Nobody could contradict that. But—maybe just because she was the best—people stopped wanting to see her dance. Another reason for this was that, after a while, her dancing began to make the people who saw it so sad that they would not want to see her twice. Word got around. Who wants to sit through an evening at the ballet with a sword of anguish piercing their heart and tears pouring down their cheeks?

Somehow, by and by, when Anna danced, all her steps and gestures, all the things she did with her arms and legs and hands and head, all these movements reminded people of griefs and worries they would prefer not to think about, of how everybody grows old and dies, of how objects get lost and forgotten, no matter how beautiful they are, of the terrible mistakes that get made, and the wrong things that people do from not taking enough trouble, how even good deeds get forgotten, and how time goes by and carries everything into the past.

So, as the years sailed on, theaters stopped inviting Anna to come and dance. Although she was the best dancer in the world, she hardly ever gave a performance. And, after a while, very few people knew whether she was alive or dead. Not even her Cousin Bert.

Nor did she know whether Bert was alive or dead— though she sometimes wondered about him, whether he still traveled about on the *Queen Anne's Lace*. And was Ulysses still with him? And had he ever found another chimney cuckoo's egg?

One spring day, Anna received an invitation to dance. It was a private request, not from a theater. A rich man, a millionaire, a Mr. Jed Fanfare, would be obliged if she would come and dance for him at his home. Any day would be convenient to him.

Anna sent a message that she would come at once, for she had no other engagements. She had herself driven in her Rolls Royce to his house in Surrey.

Mr. Fanfare was so rich that his house was patrolled by dozens of armed guards, and there were savage dogs prowling around the grounds, who could bite off your leg like a stick of licorice, and there was bullet-proof glass in the doors and windows of the house, which was quite as large as any palace. Inside, the whole place was hung with silk tapestries, and there were pictures on the walls by old, old masters, and the chairs were covered with

Chinese silk and the tables inlaid with silver and mother-of-pearl. And it was all quiet, dark and silent as the inside of a bank vault.

Anna passed the guards and was taken upstairs in a lift, then sped along a corridor on a gliding walkway; from the moment she entered the house she did not have to walk a single step. When she reached Mr. Fanfare's room she understood the reason for this: the millionaire sat in a wheelchair, paralyzed except for his eyes, which could follow her as she moved, and his eyelids, which could blink open or shut.

Thank goodness for that! Anna thought. Suppose he were unable to shut his eyes, but was obliged to sit looking at everything, whether he wanted to or not! And she thought how lucky she was, to be able to move.

When she looked a second time at Mr. Fanfare, she recognized him, though his hair had grown white and his face was pale as lard. Why, he was the rich man who had bought the first chimney cuckoo's egg at the auction, and had failed to catch it. And when Anna looked at the man who pushed the wheelchair, she recognized him too: he was the small man in the fur coat who had given her the second egg. He gave her a gentle smile and said,

"Mr. Fanfare is my brother. My name is Sam Fanfare."

Anna glanced around her. They were in a huge room with a polished wood floor and windows at the far end. Plenty of room for her to dance.

"May I have some music?" she asked.

"Of course," said Sam Fanfare. "I will put on my

brother's favorite record. Very likely you know the words."

The tune of the record was familiar to Anna, but the words were somewhat different from those she remembered.

> The cuckoo is a witty bird
> No other one is so;
> She lays her eggs at random
> Nor stays to see them grow;
> She hates the rainy winter
> She shuns the frost and snow;
> How happily with her I'd say,
> Cuckoo! Cuckoo! Cuckoo!
> And off with her I'd go!

Anna began to dance.

The tune was a cheerful one, so she tried to make her dancing lively and joyful to match it. That poor man, she thought, has paid for me to come here, to dance and cheer him. I must try to make him remember what it was like for him when he could move about freely, like a bird, like the wind.

So, in her movements, she began to imitate the wind, which carries the air along in shapes, though we can't see them; and she showed how birds fly, making use of the wind, letting it carry them, floating on it—or, sometimes, fighting it, diving through its invisible waves.

This was how Anna danced. And, for some reason, although what she was doing did not involve difficult steps, she found it terribly hard; she felt as if she were learning to dance all over again from the very beginning; she felt as if she were dancing in glue, not air; as the music went on and on she found it harder and harder.

I can't bear this, she thought. I simply cannot bear it for another minute. But I must pretend to do it as lightly and easily as if it were no effort at all.

And the struggle to do this made her heart nearly burst inside her.

I have never known before how hard it is to dance, she thought. But I must look happy. Mr. Fanfare is paying me, and he has been in a wheelchair for so many years, I must try to give him his money's worth; I must look as if I loved performing every step and twirl and pirouette.

The effort to do that was so severe that she felt great tears growing in her eyes. He must not see them, she thought, and she turned her head away and leapt into the air with the grace of a swift. Some dancers can remain off the ground, or look as if they do, for several moments at a time, lifting themselves against gravity like birds; Anna could do that.

And she did it for Mr. Fanfare, again and again.

At last the music ended. Anna felt as if she had been dancing all day and all night. She wanted to rush away, out of the room, hide her head in a pillow and cry her heart out. Instead, she curtsied formally to Mr. Fanfare, head bowed forward, arms spread sideways like the wings of a swan.

Then she saw that his eyelids were blinking, faster and faster. Tears began to run down his cheeks. His mouth began to move; it opened and closed. He turned his head; he clenched his hands. Then he spoke.

"What—what can I give you?" he croaked.

Behind Anna, she heard Sam Fanfare gasp. "My brother has not spoken for fifteen years!" he said in a whisper.

Mr. Fanfare stretched out his hands.

"What can I give you?" he said again.

"Nothing, nothing!" she cried. "There is absolutely nothing that I need!"

And now she let her own tears run; they poured down her face.

"But carry your mind back to the auction," suggested Sam Fanfare. "Supposing you had not asked what you did? Was there nothing else that you might have asked for?"

Anna took her mind back and she remembered that day.

"Yes," she said slowly. "There *is* something else. But I am afraid that it does not exist."

"Ah, but it does exist," said Sam. "My brother owns it. And now it is yours."

He rang a bell, and soon two footmen appeared carrying a basket.

"Name it yourself," croaked Mr. Fanfare, and he pushed himself out of his wheelchair and handed the basket to Anna. Then he walked to the window and looked out.

Anna went in search of her Cousin Bert. She dismissed her chauffeur and drove her own car—not the Rolls

Royce, but a little one. Bert's barge was not at Tiny Dunmow—nor at Musselboys—nor at Brentwood, Huntingdon, nor Newark—but at last, somewhere between these towns, on the canal, in a place I won't name, she found the *Queen Anne's Lace*.

From a distance, you could hardly have told that it was a barge. Moss and earth had gathered along the decks and on the cabin roof; grass and wild flowers and even hazel bushes had put down roots, had grown and flourished; the boat looked like a long section of the bank that had come adrift and was gliding along in the water. Only an occasional puff of smoke from the chimney would ever show that it was a human dwelling.

Ulysses the lion strolled back and forth on the deck. He no longer looked sick and sorrowful; his coat was thick and white as frost, his eyes shone with hope and health as he looked ahead. Ulysses was not the only animal on the barge; there were red squirrels in the hazel bushes, and hedgehogs in the grass, and lizards in the cracks of the wood, and a badger put its head out of the hatch. There were swifts nesting above the windows and a barn owl perched on a coil of rope. There were ducks on the roof and a goat on the coaming and a grass-snake sunning itself by a clump of primroses.

"Ahoy!" called Anna. "Ahoy there, Bert Fern! Are you on board?"

She had parked her car by a pair of lock gates, and stood on the bank holding the basket.

Bert's rusty head appeared in the cabin doorway. There

were some streaks of gray in the rust now, which did not surprise Anna. There were gray streaks in her own hair, which had once been black as jet.

Bert did not seem too surprised to see his cousin.

"Well, there, Annie!" he said comfortably. "You're in nice time for breakfast. I was just going to make the porridge."

For it was still early, six in the morning. Anna had been driving all night.

"I've brought you an Easter gift, Bert," she said. "It's for Ulysses, really."

She jumped on board and opened the basket. Out of it climbed a snowy white lion cub, which Ulysses at once began to lick in a friendly way.

"Her name's Penelope," said Anna.

"Fed up with dancing, are you, Annie?" said Bert, as he gave her a bowl of porridge.

"Well," said she, "no, not fed up, exactly—I'll always go on dancing, as long as I can, but I'll do other things as well, like maybe travel about with you on the *Queen Anne's Lace*. If you'll have me."

"And welcome," said Bert. "Full ship we'll be. See what I found in the ashes this morning when I raked out the stove."

He fetched a bowl of moss, which he had set in a sunny corner, and showed her two chimney cuckoos' eggs.

Miss Hooting's
Legacy

For weeks before Cousin Elspeth's visit Mrs. Armitage was, as her son Mark put it, "flapping about like a wet sheet in a bramble bush."

"What shall we do about the unicorn? Cousin Elspeth doesn't approve of keeping pets."

"But she can't disapprove of him. He's got an angelic nature—haven't you, Candleberry?"

Harriet patted the unicorn and gave him a lump of sugar. It was a hot day in early October and the family were having tea in the garden.

"He'll have to board out for a month or two at Cold-harbor Farm." Mrs. Armitage made a note on her list. "And you," she said to her husband, "must lay in at least five cases of Glensporran. Cousin Elspeth will only drink iced tea with whisky in it."

"Merciful powers! What this visit is going to cost us! How long is the woman going to stay?"

"Why does she have to come?" growled Mark, who

had been told to dismantle his homemade nuclear turbine, which was just outside the guest room window.

"Because she's a poor old thing and her sister's just died, and she's lonely. Also, she's very rich, and if she felt like it, she could easily pay for you and Harriet to go to college, or art school, or something of that sort."

"But that's *years* ahead!"

"*Someone* has to think ahead in this family," said Mrs. Armitage, writing down *Earl Grey tea, new face towels* on her list. "And, Harriet, you are not to encourage the cat to come upstairs and sleep on your bed. It would be awful if he got into Cousin Elspeth's room and disturbed her. She writes that she is a very light sleeper—"

"Oh, poor Walrus. Where *can* he sleep, then?"

"In his basket, in the kitchen. And, Mark, will you ask Mr. Peake to stay out of the guest bathroom for a few months? He's very obliging, but it always takes a long time to get an idea into his head."

"Well, he *is* three hundred years old, after all," said Harriet. "You can't expect a ghost to respond quite as quickly as ordinary people."

"Darling," said Mrs. Armitage to her husband, "sometime this week, could you find a few minutes to hang up the big mirror that I bought at Dowbridges' sale? It's been down in the cellar for the last two months—"

"Hang it, where?" said Mr. Armitage, reluctantly coming out of his evening paper.

"In the guest room, of course! To replace the one that Mark broke when his turbine exploded—"

"I'll do it, if you like," said Mark, who loved banging in nails. "After all, it was my fault the other one got broken."

"And I'll help," said Harriet, who wanted another look at the new mirror.

She had accompanied her mother to the furniture sale a couple of months ago, when three linen tablecloths, one wall mirror, ten flowerpots, and a rusty pressure cooker had been sold to Mrs. Armitage for twelve pounds in the teeth of spirited and urgent bidding from old Miss Hooting, who lived at the other end of the village. For some reason the old lady seemed particularly keen to acquire this lot, though there were several other mirrors in the sale. At £11.99, however, she ceased to wave her umbrella, and limped out of the sale hall, scowling, muttering, and casting angry glances at Mrs. Armitage. Since then she had twice dropped notes, in black spidery handwriting, through the Armitage letterbox offering to buy the mirror, first for £12.50, then for £13, but Mrs. Armitage, who did not much like Miss Hooting, politely declined to sell.

"I wonder *why* the old girl was so keen to get hold of the glass?" remarked Harriet, holding the jar full of nails while Mark tapped exploringly on the wall, hunting for reliable spots. The mirror was quite a big heavy one, about four feet long by two feet wide, and required careful positioning.

"It seems ordinary enough." Mark glanced at it casually. The glass, plainly quite old, had a faint silvery sheen; the frame, wooden and very worn, was carved with vine leaves and little grinning creatures.

"It doesn't give a very good reflection." Harriet peered in. "Makes me look frightful."

"Oh, I dunno; about the same as usual, I'd say," remarked her brother. He selected his spot, pressed a nail into the plaster, and gave it one or two quick bangs. "There. Now another here. Now pass us the glass."

They heard the doorbell ring as Mark hung up the mirror, and a few minutes later, when they came clattering downstairs with the hammer and nails and the stepladder, they saw their mother on the doorstep, engrossed in a long, earnest conversation with old Mrs. Lomax, Miss Hooting's neighbor. Mrs. Lomax was not a close friend of the Armitage family, but she had once obligingly restored the Armitage parents to their proper shape when Miss Hooting, in a fit of temper, had changed them into ladybirds.

Odd things frequently happened to the Armitages.

"What did Mrs. Lomax want, Ma?" Harriet asked her mother at supper.

Mrs. Armitage frowned, looking half worried, half annoyed.

"It's still this business about the mirror," she said. "Old Miss Hooting had really set her heart on it, for some reason. Why didn't she just *tell* me so? Now she has got pneumonia. She's quite ill, Mrs. Lomax says, and she keeps tossing and turning, and saying she has to have the glass, and if not, she'll put a curse on us by dropping a bent pin down our well. Perhaps, after all, I had better let the poor old thing have the glass."

"Why? You bought it," said Harriet. "She could have gone on bidding."

"Perhaps £11.99 was all she had."

"There were other glasses that went for less."

Mr. Armitage was inclined to make light of the matter. "I don't see what dropping a bent pin into the well could do. I expect she's delirious. Wait till she's better; then you'll find the whole thing has died down, very likely."

Next day, however, the Armitages learned that old Miss Hooting had died in the night.

"And not before it was time," said Mr. Armitage. "She must have been getting on for a hundred. Anyway, that solves your problem about the mirror."

"I hope so," said his wife.

"Now all we have to worry about is Cousin Elspeth. Did you say she takes cubes of frozen tea in her whisky, or frozen whisky in her tea?"

"Either way will do, so long as the tea is Earl Grey . . ."

Cousin Elspeth's arrival coincided with old Miss Hooting's funeral.

The funeral of a witch (or "old fairy lady" as they were always politely referred to in the Armitages' village, where a great many of them resided) is always a solemn affair, and Miss Hooting, because of her great age and explosive temper, had generally been regarded as the chairwitch of the village community. So the hearse, drawn by four black griffins and carrying a glass coffin with Miss Hooting in it, looking very severe in her black robes and hat, was followed by a long straggling procession of other old ladies, riding in vehicles of all kinds, from rickety perch phaetons with half the springs gone, to moth-eaten flying carpets and down-at-the-wheel chariots.

Mark and Harriet would very much have liked to attend the ceremony, but were told firmly that, since the family had not been on very good terms with Miss Hooting, they were to stay at home and not intrude. They heard later from their friend Rosie Perrow that there had been a considerable fuss at the graveside, because Miss Hooting had left instructions that her coffin was not to be covered over until November first, and the vicar had very strong objections to this.

"Especially as the coffin was made of glass," Rosie reported.

"I suppose he thought kids might come and smash it," said Mark.

"So they might. Miss Hooting wasn't at all popular."

Cousin Elspeth, when she arrived, was in a state of high indignation.

"Rickety, ramshackle equipages all along the village street, holding up the traffic! My taxi took twenty-eight minutes to get here, and cost me £9.83! Furrthermore, I am accustomed to take my tea at four-thirty preecisely, and it is now twelve meenutes past five!"

Cousin Elspeth was a tall, rangy lady, with teeth that Mr. Armitage said reminded him of the cliffs of Dover, a voice like a chain saw, cold, granite-colored eyes that missed nothing, hair like the English Channel on a gray choppy day, and an Aberdeen accent as frigid as chopped ice.

In a way, Mark thought, it was a shame that she had just missed Miss Hooting; the two of them might have hit it off.

Tea, with three kinds of scones, two kinds of shortbread, and cubes of frozen Glensporran in her Earl Grey, was just beginning to soothe Cousin Elspeth's ruffled feelings when there came a peal at the front doorbell.

"Inconseederate!" Cousin Elspeth sniffed again.

The caller proved to be Mr. Glibchick, the senior partner in the legal firm of Wright, Wright, Wright, Wright, and Wrong, who had their offices on the village green. All the Wrights and the Wrongs had long since passed away, and Mr. Glibchick ran the firm with the help of his junior partner, Mr. Wrangle.

"What was it, dear?" inquired Mrs. Armitage, when her husband returned, looking rather astonished, from his conversation with the lawyer.

"Just imagine—Miss Hooting has left us something in her Will!"

Cousin Elspeth was all ears at once. Making and re-making her own Will had been her favorite hobby for years past, and since arriving at the Armitage house she had already mentally subtracted £400 and a writing desk from Mark's legacy, because he had neglected to pass her the jam, and was deliberating at present about whether to bequeath a favorite brown mohair stole to Harriet, who had politely inquired after her lumbago.

"Left us a legacy? What—in the name of goodness?" exclaimed Mrs. Armitage. "I thought the poor old thing hadn't two pennies to rub together."

"Not money. Two mechanical helots, was what Mr. Glibchick said."

"Helots? What are they?"

"Helots were a kind of slave."

"Fancy Miss Hooting keeping slaves!" Harriet looked horrified. "I bet she beat them with her umbrella and made them live on burnt toast crusts."

"Little gels should be seen and not hairrd," remarked Cousin Elspeth, giving Harriet a disapproving glance, and changing her mind about the brown mohair stole.

Next day the mechanical slaves were delivered by Ernie Perrow in his tractor-trailer.

They proved to be two figures, approximately human in shape, one rather larger than life-size, one rather smaller, constructed out of thin metal piping, with plastic boxes for their chests containing a lot of electronic gadgetry. Their feet were large, round, and heavy, and they had long multi-hinged arms ending in prehensile hands with hooks on the fingers. They had eyes made of electric light bulbs and rather vacant expressions. Their names were stenciled on their feet: *Tinthea* and *Nickelas*.

"What gruesome objects!" exclaimed Mrs. Armitage.

"For mercy's sake, let's give them to the next church sale; the very sight of them is enough to give me one of my migraines!"

Cousin Elspeth entirely agreed. "Whit seengularly reepulsive airrticles!"

But Mark and his father, seeing eye to eye for once, were most anxious to get the mechanical slaves into working order, if possible.

"Besides, it would be most tactless to give them to a sale. Miss Hooting's friends would be sure to get to know."

"The things are in a horrible condition," pronounced Mark, after some study of the helots. "All damp and dirty and rusty; the old girl must have kept them in some dismal outhouse and never oiled them."

"What makes them go?" inquired Harriet, peering at a damp, tattered little booklet, entitled *Component Identification*, which hung on a chain around Tinthea's neck.

"It seems to be lunar energy," said her father. "Which is pretty dicey, if you ask me. I never heard of anything running on lunar energy before. But that seems to be the purpose of those glass plates on the tops of their heads."

"More to 'em than meets the eye," agreed Mark, wagging his own head.

As it happened, the month of October was very fine. Hot, sunny days were succeeded by blazing moonlit nights. Tinthea and Nickelas were put out in the greenhouse to warm up and dry off. Meanwhile Mark and his father, each guided by a booklet, spent devoted hours cleaning, drying, oiling and de-rusting the family's new possessions.

" 'Clean glazed areas with water and ammonia solution,' it says."

" 'Brush cassette placement with household detergent.' "

"Which is the cassette placement?"

"I think it must be that drawer affair in the chest."

"Chest of drawers," giggled Harriet.

Tinthea, on whom Mark was working, let out something that sounded like a snort.

" 'Keep latched prehensile work/monitor selector function aligners well lubricated with sunflower or cottonseed oil.' Which do you think those are?"

"Its hands?" suggested Harriet.

Mr. Armitage, doing his best to clean the feet of Nickelas, which were in a shocking state, matted with dirt and old, encrusted furniture polish, accidentally touched a concealed lever in the heel, and Nickelas began to hop about, in a slow, ungainly, but frantic way, like a toad in a bed of thistles. The helot's hand, convulsively opening and shutting, grasped the handle of Mr. Armitage's metal toolbox, picked up the box, and swung it at its owner's head. Mr. Armitage just managed to save himself from a cracked skull by falling over sideways into a tray of flowerpots. Nickelas then clumsily but effectively smashed eight greenhouse panes with the end of the toolbox, using it like a sledgehammer, before Mark, ducking low, managed to grab the helot's leg and flick down the switch.

"Oh, I see, *that's* how they work!" Harriet pressed Tinthea's switch.

"Don't, idiot!" shouted Mark, but it was too late. Tinthea picked up a bucket of dirty, soapy water and dashed it into Harriet's face just before Mr. Armitage, with great presence of mind, hooked the helot's feet from under her with the end of a rake. Tinthea fell flat on the ground, and Mark was able to switch her off.

"We have got to learn to program them properly before we switch them on. They seem to have charged up quite a lot of lunar energy," said Mr. Armitage, trying to prize Nickelas's steel fingers loose from the handle of the tool-chest.

He read aloud: " 'To program the helots: turn the percept/accept/monitor/selector to zero. If the helot is in multiple cycle, depress the Clear key. The memory will then return to Stage 0½. Bring the memory factor into play by raising shutter of display window, simultaneously depressing locking lever, opening upper assembly carriage masker, sliding drum axle out of tab rack, shifting wheel track chain into B position, and moving present button to ←⟩ signal. Is that clear?" said Mr. Armitage, after a little thought.

"No," said Mark. "Do these things have memories then?"

"I think so. I'm not quite sure about that Stage 0½. Maybe they still have some instructions programmed into them by old Miss Hooting. I'm not quite sure how to get rid of those. Here, it says, 'The helot will remember the previous day's instructions and repeat for an indefinite number of operations unless the memory factor is cancelled by opening "R" slot and simultaneously depressing all function keys.' I must say," said Mr. Armitage, suddenly becoming enthusiastic, "if we could get Nickelas, for instance, to take over all the digging and lawn mowing, and carry the garbage bin to the street, I should be quite grateful to old Miss Hooting for her legacy, and I'm sorry I ever called her a troublemaking old so-and-so."

"And maybe we can program Tinthea to wash dishes and make beds?" Harriet suggested hopefully.

But there was a long way to go before the helots could be set to perform any useful task with the slightest certainty that it would be carried out properly.

Tinthea, programmed to make the beds, showered sunflower oil liberally all over the blankets, and then tore up the sheets into shreds; she finished by scooping handfuls of foam rubber out of the mattresses, and unstringing all the bedsprings. The only bed spared was that of Cousin Elspeth, who always kept her bedroom door locked. Tinthea was unable to get into her room, though she returned to rattle vainly at the door handle all day long.

Nickelas, meanwhile, ran amok with the motor mower, trundling it back and forth across the garden, laying flat all Mrs. Armitage's begonias and dahlias in fifteen minutes; Mark was able to lasso him and switch him off just before he began on the sweet peas.

"We'd better get rid of them before they murder us all in our beds," said Mrs. Armitage.

"It seems a shame not to get *some* use out of them," said Harriet. "Don't you think we could teach Tinthea to do the cooking?"

But Tinthea's notion of cooking was to pile every article from the refrigerator into the oven, including ice cubes and Mr. Armitage's special film for his Japanese camera. And then Harriet found her supplying buckets of strong Earl Grey tea to Nickelas, who was pouring them over Mr. Armitage's cherished asparagus bed.

Instructed to pick blackberries for jam, Nickelas came back with a basket containing enough Deadly Nightshade berries to poison the entire village. Tinthea, set to polish the stairs, covered them with salad oil; Harriet was just in time to catch Cousin Elspeth as she slid down the last six steps. The results of this were quite advantageous, for Harriet was, on the spot, reappointed to the brown mohair stole in Cousin Elspeth's Will (though not informed of the fact) and Cousin Elspeth's lumbago, as it proved subsequently, was cured forever by the shock of the fall; but everybody in the household began to feel that the helots were more of a liability than an asset.

But how to dispose of them?

"If I were ye, I'd smesh 'em with a hetchit," snapped Cousin Elspeth.

"I don't think *that* would be advisable. A witch's legacy, you know, should be treated with caution."

"A witch! Hech!"

Mr. Armitage telephoned the local museum to ask if they would accept the helots; but Mr. Muskin, the curator, was away for a month in Tasmania, collecting ethnological curiosities. The nearest National Trust mansion had to refer the possibility of being given two lunar-powered helots to its Acquisitions Board; and the librarian at the village library was quite certain she didn't want them; nor did the Primary School.

For the time, Tinthea and Nickelas were locked in the cellar. "They won't pick up much lunar power there," said Mr. Armitage. They could be heard gloomily thumping about from time to time.

"I think they must have learned how to switch each other on," said Mark.

"It's a bit spooky having them down there," shivered Harriet. "I wish Mr. Muskin would come back from Tasmania and decide to have them."

Meanwhile, to everybody's amazement, a most remarkable change was taking place in Cousin Elspeth. This was so noticeable, and so wholly unexpected, that it even distracted the family's attention from the uncertainty of having two somewhat unbiddable helots in the cellar.

In fact, as Mr. Armitage said to his wife, it was almost impossible to believe the evidence of one's own eyes.

In the course of three weeks Cousin Elspeth's looks and her temper improved daily and visibly. Her cheeks grew pink, her eyes blue, and her face no longer looked like a craggy mountain landscape, but became simply handsome and distinguished. She was heard to laugh, several times, and told Mrs. Armitage that it didn't matter if the tea wasn't always Earl Grey; she remembered a limerick she had heard in her youth about the Old Man of Hoy, restored the writing desk to Mark in her Will, and began to leave her bedroom door unlocked.

Curiously enough, after a week or two, it was Mrs. Armitage who began to think rather wistfully of the wasted helot manpower lying idle down there in the cellar. She told Mark to fetch Tinthea to help with the job of washing blankets, which Cousin Elspeth pointed out should be done before the winter.

"After all, as we've got the creatures we might as well make *some* use of them. Just carrying blankets to and fro, Tinthea can't get up to much mischief. But don't bring Nickelas, I can't stand his big staring eyes."

So Mark, assisted by Harriet, fetched the smaller helot from the cellar. They were careful not to switch her on until she was in the utility room, and the cellar door locked again on the inert Nickelas.

But Harriet did afterward recall that Tinthea's bulbous, sightless eyes seemed to watch the process of locking and unlocking very attentively.

For once, however, the smaller helot appeared to be in a cooperative mood, and she hoisted wet blankets out of the washing machine and trundled off with them into the garden, where she hung them on the line without doing anything unprogrammed or uncalled-for, returning three or four times for a new load. It was bright, blowy autumn weather, the leaves were whirling off the trees, and the blankets dried so quickly that they were ready to put back on the beds after a couple of hours.

"Ech! Bless my soul!" sighed Cousin Elspeth at tea, which was, again, taken in the garden as the weather was so fine. "This veesit has passed so quickly, it's harrd to realize that it will be November on Thurrsday. I must be thinking of reeturrning to my ain wee naist."

"Oh, but you mustn't think of leaving before our Halloween party," said Mrs. Armitage quickly. "We have *so* much enjoyed having you, Cousin Elspeth, you must make this visit an annual event. It has been a real pleasure."

"Indeed it has! I've taken a grand fancy to your young folk." Cousin Elspeth beamed benevolently at Mark and Harriet, who were lying on their stomachs on the grass, doing homework between bites of bread and damson jam.

"Where's Tinthea?" Harriet suddenly said to Mark. "Did you put her away?"

"No, I didn't. Did you?"

Harriet shook her head.

Quietly she and Mark rose, left the group around the garden table, and went indoors.

"I can hear something upstairs," said Mark.

A thumping could be heard from the direction of Cousin Elspeth's room.

Harriet armed herself with a broom, Mark picked a

walking stick from the umbrella stand, and they hurried up the stairs.

As they entered Cousin Elspeth's room, Tinthea could be seen apparently admiring herself in the large looking glass. Then, advancing to it with outstretched monitor selection function aligners, she was plainly about to remove it from the wall when Mark, stepping forward, tapped down her main switch with the ferule of the walking stick. Tinthea let out what sounded like a cry of rage and spun half round before she lost her power and became inert, with dangling mandibles and vacant receiving panel; but even so it seemed to Harriet that there was a very malevolent expression in her sixty-watt eyes.

"What was *really* queer, though," Harriet said to her brother, "was that just before you hooked down her switch I caught sight of her reflection in the glass, and she looked—well, not like a helot, more like a person. There *is* something peculiar about that mirror."

She studied herself in the glass.

"The first time I saw myself in it I thought I looked horrible. But now I look better. . . ."

Mark eyed his reflection and said, "Perhaps that's what's been happening to Cousin Elspeth; seeing herself in the glass day after day . . . "

"Of *course*! Aren't you clever! So that's why old Miss Hooting wanted it! But what shall we do about Tinthea?"

"Put her back in the cellar. You take her legs. Don't touch the switch." Tinthea sagged heavily between them as they carried her back to the cellar. And when she was set down next to Nickelas, it seemed to Harriet that a wordless message flashed between the two bulbous pairs of sightless eyes.

The Armitages' Halloween party was always a great success.

This year Mrs. Armitage, with Cousin Elspeth and Harriet helping, produced a magnificent feast, including several Scottish delicacies such as haggis and Aberdeen Bun; Mark and Harriet organized apple bobbing, table turning, and fortune telling with tea leaves (large Earl Grey ones), flour, lighted candles, and soot. The guests came dressed as trolls, kelpies, banshees, werewolves, or boggarts, and the sensation of the evening was the pair of helots, Tinthea and Nickelas, who, carefully and lengthily programmed during days of hard work by Mr. Armitage, passed around trays of cheese tarts, chestnut crunch fancies, and tiny curried sausages.

"But they're not real, are they?" cried Mrs. Pontwell, the vicar's wife. "I mean—they are Mark and Harriet, cleverly dressed up, aren't they, really?"

When she discovered that the helots were *not* Mark and Harriet she gave a slight scream and kept well out of their way for the rest of the evening.

Many of the guests remained, playing charades, until nearly midnight, but Cousin Elspeth, who intended to leave the following morning, retired to bed at half past ten.

"Och! I've just had a grand time," she said. "I never thocht I'd enjoy a party so well. But old bones, ye ken, need plainty of rest; I'll e'en take maself off to ma wee bed, for I must be up bricht and airrly the morn."

Her absence did not diminish the gaiety of the party, and Mrs. Armitage was serving cups of hot chocolate with rum in it while everybody sang "Widecombe Fair," when piercing shrieks were heard from upstairs. Simultaneously all the lights went out.

"Och, maircy! Mairder! Mairder! Mairder!"

"Sounds as if someone's strangling Cousin Elspeth," said Mark, starting for the stairs.

"Where did you put the matches?" said Harriet.

There were plenty of candles and matches lying around, but in the confusion, with guests and members of the family bumping about in the dark, it was some time before a rescue party, consisting of Mark, Mr. Armitage, and Mr. Shepherd from next door, was able to mount the stairs with candles and make their way to Cousin Elspeth's room.

They found that lady sitting up in bed in shawl and nightcap, almost paralytic with indignation.

"A deedy lot you are, upon my worrd! I could have been torrn leemb fra leemb before ye lifted a feenger!"

"But what happened?" said Mr. Armitage, looking around in perplexity.

"The mirror's gone!" said Mark.

"Whit happened? Whit *happened?* Yon unco' mis-shapen stravaiging shilpit monsters of yours cam'

45

glomping intil ma room—bauld as brass!—removed the meerror fra the wall, and glomped off oot again, as calm as Plato! Wheer they have taken it, I dinna speer—nor do I care—but thankful I am this is the last nicht in life I'll pass under *this* roof, and I'll ne'er come back afore death bears me awa', and it's only a wonder I didna die on the spot wi' petrification!" And Cousin Elspeth succumbed to a fit of violent hysterics, needing to be ministered to with burnt feathers, sal volatile, brandy, snuff, hotwater bottles and antiphlogistine poultices.

While this was happening, Mark said to Harriet, "Where do you suppose the helots have taken the mirror?"

"Back to the cellar? How did they get out?"

By this time most of the guests had gone. The blown fuse had been mended and the lights restored. Mark and Harriet went down, a little cautiously, to inspect the cellar, but found it empty; the lock had been neatly picked from inside.

As they returned to the hall the telephone rang. Mark picked up the receiver and heard the vicar's voice.

"Mark, is that you, my boy? I'm afraid those two mechanical monsters of yours are up to something very fishy in the churchyard. I can see them from my study window in the moonlight. Will you ask your father to come along, and tell him I've phoned P.C. Loiter."

"Oh, *now* what?" groaned Mr. Armitage on hearing this news, but he accompanied his children to the churchyard, which was only a five-minute run along the village street, leaving Mrs. Armitage in charge of the stricken Cousin Elspeth.

A large bright hunter's moon was sailing overhead, and by its light it was easy to see Nickelas and Tinthea hoisting up Miss Hooting's glass coffin. They had excavated the grave with amazing speed, and now carefully placed the coffin on the grass to one side of it. Then they laid the mirror, reflecting surface down, on top of the coffin.

As the Armitages arrived at one gate, the vicar and P.C. Loiter came from the vicarage garden.

"Here! What's going on!" shouted P.C. Loiter, out-raged. "Just you stop that—whatever you're doing! If you ask me," he added in an undertone to Mr. Pontwell, "that's what comes of burying these here wit—these old fairy ladies in churchyards along with decent folk."

"Oh, dear me," said the vicar, "but we must be broad-minded, you know, and Miss Hooting had been such a long-established member of our community—"

At this moment Nickelas and Tinthea, taking no notice of P.C. Loiter's shouts, raised the mirror high above the coffin, holding it like a canopy.

"What's the idea, d'you suppose?" Mark muttered to Harriet.

"So as to get the reflection of Miss Hooting inside the coffin—"

"Ugh!"

The coffin suddenly exploded with the kind of noise that a gas oven makes when somebody has been too slow

47

in lighting the match. The helots fell backward, letting go of the mirror, which fell and smashed.

A large owl was seen to fly away from where the coffin had been.

P.C. Loiter, very reluctantly, but encouraged by the presence of Mr. Pontwell and Mr. Armitage on either side, went forward and inspected the coffin. But there was nothing in it, except a great deal of broken glass. Nor was the body of Miss Hooting ever seen again.

"I think it was a plan that went wrong," said Harriet to Mark. "I think she hoped, if she had the mirror, it would make her young and handsome and stop her from dying."

"So she sent the helots to get it? Maybe," said Mark.

"What a shame the mirror got smashed. Because, look at Cousin Elspeth!"

Cousin Elspeth, overnight, had gone back to exactly what she had been at the beginning of the visit—sour, dour, hard-featured, and extremely bad-tempered.

"Ye might have provided a drap of Earl Grey for my last breakfast!" she snapped. "And, as for that disgreeceful occurrence last nicht—aweel, the less said the better!" After which she went on to say a great deal more about it, and, as she left, announced that Mark would certainly not get the writing desk nor Harriet the mohair stole, since they were undoubtedly responsible for the goings-on in the night.

"Somehow I don't see Cousin Elspeth putting us through

art school," mused Harriet, as the taxi rolled away with their cousin along the village street.

"That's a long way off," said Mark peacefully.

Mr. Armitage was on the telephone to Dowbridges, the auctioneers.

"I want you to come and fetch two robots and enter them in your Friday sale. Please send a truck at once; I'd like them out of the house by noon. Yes, *robots*; two lunar-powered robots, in full working order, complete with instruction booklets. Handy for workshop, kitchen, or garden; a really useful pair; you can price the large one at £90 and the small at £50."

On Friday Mrs. Armitage and Harriet attended the sale, and returned to report with high satisfaction that both helots had been sold to old Admiral Lycanthrop.

"*He'll* give them what-for, I bet," said Mark. "*He* won't stand any nonsense from them."

But, alas, it turned out that the admiral, who was rather hard of hearing, thought he was bidding for two rowboats, and when he discovered that his purchase consisted instead of two lunar-powered mechanical slaves with awkward dispositions, he returned them, demanding his money back.

The Armitages came down to breakfast on Saturday to find Nickelas and Tinthea standing mute, dogged, and expectant, outside the back door. . . .

The Gift Giving

The weeks leading up to Christmas were always full of excitement, and tremendous anxiety too, as the family waited in suspense for the Uncles, who had set off in the spring of the year, to return from their summer's traveling and trading: Uncle Emer, Uncle Acraud, Uncle Gonfil, and Uncle Mark. They always started off together, down the steep mountainside, but then, at the bottom, they took different routes along the deep narrow valley, Uncle Mark and Uncle Acraud riding eastward, toward the great plains, while Uncle Emer and Uncle Gonfil turned west, toward the towns and rivers and the western sea.

Then, before they were clear of the mountains, they would separate once more, Uncle Acraud turning south, Uncle Emer taking his course northward, so that, the children occasionally thought, their family was scattered over the whole world, netted out like a spider's web.

Spring, summer would go by, in the usual occupations, digging and sowing the steep hillside garden beds, fishing, hunting for hares, picking wild strawberries, making hay. Then, toward St. Drimma's Day, when the winds began to blow and the snow crept down, lower and lower, from the high peaks, Grandmother would begin to grow restless.

Silent and calm all summer long she sat in her rocking chair on the wide wooden porch, wrapped in a patchwork comforter, with her blind eyes turned eastward toward the lands where Mark, her dearest and first-born, had gone. But when the winds of Michaelmas began to blow, and the wolves grew bolder, and the children dragged in sacks of logs day after day, and the cattle were brought down to the stable under the house, then Grandmother grew agitated indeed.

When Sammle, the eldest granddaughter, brought her hot milk, she would grip the girl's slender brown wrist and demand: "Tell me, child, how many days now to St. Froida's Day?" (which was the first of December).

"Eighteen, Grandmother," Sammle would answer, stooping to kiss the wrinkled cheek.

"So many, still? So many till we may hope to see them?"

"Don't worry, Granny, the Uncles are *certain* to return safely. Perhaps they will be early this year. Perhaps we may see them before the Feast of St. Melin" (which was December the fourteenth).

And then, sure enough, sometime during the middle weeks of December, their great carts would come jingling and trampling along the winding valleys. Young Mark (son of Uncle Emer), from his watchpoint up a tall pine over a high cliff, would catch the flash of a baggage-mule's brass brow-medal, or the sun glancing on the barrel of a carbine, and would come joyfully dashing back to report.

"Granny! Granny! The Uncles are almost here!"

Then the whole household, the whole village, would be filled with as much agitation and turmoil as that of a kingdom of ants when the spade breaks open their hummock; wives would build the fires higher, and fetch out the best linen, wine, dried meat, pickled eggs; set dough to rising, mix cakes of honey and oats, bring up stone jars of preserved strawberries from the cellars; and the children, with the servants and half the village, would go racing down the perilous zigzag track to meet the cavalcade at the bottom.

The track was far too steep for the heavy carts, which would be dismissed, and the carters paid off to go about their business; then with laughter and shouting, amid a million questions from the children, the loads would be divided and carried up the mountainside on muleback, or on human shoulders. Sometimes the Uncles came home at night, through falling snow, by the smoky light of torches; but the children and the household always knew of their arrival beforehand, and were always there to meet them.

"Did you bring Granny's Chinese shawl, Uncle Mark? Uncle Emer, have you the enameled box for her snuff that Aunt Grippa begged you to get? Uncle Acraud, did you find the glass candlesticks? Uncle Gonfil, did you bring the books?"

"Yes, yes, keep calm, don't deafen us! Poor tired travelers that we are, leave us in peace to climb this devilish hill! Everything is there, set your minds at rest—the shawl, the box, the books—besides a few other odds and ends, pins and needles and fruit and a bottle or two of wine, and a few trifles for the village. Now, just give us a few minutes to get our breath, will you, kindly—" as the children danced round them, helping each other with the smaller bundles, never ceasing to pour out questions: "Did you see the Grand Cham? The Akond of Swat? The Fon of Bikom? The Seljuk of Rum? Did you go to Cathay? To Muskovy? To Dalai? Did you travel by ship, by camel, by llama, by elephant?"

And, at the top of the hill, Grandmother would be waiting for them, out on her roofed porch, no matter how wild the weather or how late the hour, seated in majesty with her furs and patchwork quilt around her, while the Aunts ran to and fro with hot stones to place under her feet. And the Uncles always embraced her first, very fondly and respectfully, before turning to hug their wives and sisters-in-law.

Then the goods they had brought would be distributed through the village—the scissors, tools, medicines, plants, bales of cloth, ingots of metal, cordials, firearms, and musical instruments; then there would be a great feast.

Not until Christmas morning did Grandmother and the children receive the special gifts which had been brought for them by the Uncles; and this giving always took the same ceremonial form.

Uncle Mark stood behind Grandmother's chair, playing on a small pipe that he had acquired somewhere during his travels; it was made from hard black polished wood, with silver stops, and it had a mouthpiece made of amber. Uncle Mark invariably played the same tune on it at these times, very softly. It was a tune which he had heard for the first time, he said, when he was much younger, once when he had narrowly escaped falling into a crevasse on the hillside, and a voice had spoken to him, as it seemed, out of the mountain itself, bidding him watch where he set his feet and have a care, for the family depended on him. It was a gentle, thoughtful tune, which reminded Sandri, the middle granddaughter, of springtime sounds, warm wind, water from melted snow dripping off the gabled roofs, birds trying out their mating calls.

While Uncle Mark played on his pipe, Uncle Emer would hand each gift to Grandmother. And she—here was the strange thing—she, who was stone blind all the year long, could not see her own hand in front of her face—she would take the object in her fingers and instantly identify it.

"A mother-of-pearl comb, with silver studs, for Tassy . . . it comes from Babylon; a silk shawl, blue and rose, from Hind, for Argilla; a wooden game, with ivory pegs, for young Emer, from Damascus; a gold brooch, from Hangku, for Grippa; a book of rhymes, from Paris, for Sammle, bound in a scarlet leather cover."

Grandmother, who lived all the year round in darkness, could, by stroking each gift with her old, blotched, claw-like fingers, frail as quills, discover not only what the thing was and where it came from, but also the color of it, and that in the most precise and particular manner, correct to a shade.

"It is a jacket of stitched and pleated cotton, printed over with leaves and flowers; it comes from the island of Haranati, in the eastern ocean; the colors are leaf-brown and gold and a dark, dark blue, darker than mountain gentians—" for Grandmother had not always been blind; when she was a young girl she had been able to see as well as anybody else.

"And this is for you, Mother, from your son Mark," Uncle Emer would say, handing her a tissue-wrapped bundle, and she would exclaim,

"Ah, how beautiful! A coat of tribute silk, of the very palest green, so that the color shows only in the folds, like shadows on snow; the buttons and the button-toggles are of worked silk, lavender-gray, like pearl, and the stiff collar is embroidered with white roses."

"Put it on, Mother!" her sons and daughters-in-law would urge her, and the children, dancing around her chair, clutching their own treasures, would chorus, "Yes, put it on, put it on! Ah, you look like a queen, Granny, in that beautiful coat! The highest queen in the world! The queen of the mountain!"

———

Those months after Christmas were Grandmother's happiest time. Secure, thankful, with her sons safe at home, she would sit in a warm fireside corner of the big wooden family room. The wind might shriek, the snow gather higher and higher out of doors, but that did not concern her, for her family, and all the village, were well supplied with flour, oil, firewood, meat, herbs, and roots; the children had their books and toys; they learned lessons with the old priest, or made looms and spinning wheels, carved stools and chairs and chests, with the tools their uncles had brought them. The Uncles rested, and told tales of their travels; Uncle Mark played his pipe for hours together, Uncle Acraud drew pictures in charcoal of the places he had seen, and Granny, laying her hand on the paper covered with lines, would expound while Uncle Mark played:

"A huge range of mountains, like wrinkled brown linen across the horizon; a wide plain of sand, silvery blond in color, with patches of pale, pale blue; I think it is not water but air the color of water; here are strange lines across the sand where men once plowed it, long, long ago; and a great patch of crystal green, with what seems like a road crossing it; now here is a smaller region of plum-pink, bordered by an area of rusty red; I think these are the colors of the earth in these territories; it is very high up, dry from height, and the soil glittering with little particles of metal."

"You have described it better than I could myself!"

Uncle Acraud would exclaim, while the children, breathless with wonder and curiosity, sat crosslegged around her chair.

And she would answer, "Yes, but I cannot see it at all, Acraud, unless your eyes have seen it first, and I cannot see it without Mark's music to help me."

"How does Grandmother *do* it?" the children would demand of their mothers.

And Argilla, or Grippa, or Tassy, would answer, "Nobody knows. It is Grandmother's gift. She alone can do it."

The people of the village might come in, whenever they chose, and on many evenings thirty or forty would be there, silently listening, and when Grandmother retired to bed, which she did early, for the seeing made her weary, the audience would turn to one another with deep sighs, and murmur, "The world is indeed a wide place."

But with the first signs of spring the Uncles would become restless again, and begin looking over their equipment, discussing maps and routes, mending saddlebags and boots, gazing up at the high peaks for signs that the snow was in retreat.

Then Granny would grow very silent. She never asked them to stay longer, she never disputed their going, but her face seemed to shrivel, she grew smaller, wizened and huddled inside her quilted patchwork.

And on St. Petrag's Day, when they set off, when the

farewells were said and they clattered off down the mountain, through the melting snow and the trees with pink luminous buds, Grandmother would fall into a silence that lasted, sometimes, for as much as five or six weeks; all day she would sit with her face turned to the east, wordless, motionless, and would drink her milk and go to her bedroom at night still silent and dejected; it took the warm sun and sweet wild hyacinths of May to raise her spirits.

Then, by degrees, she would grow animated, and begin to say, "Only six months, now, till they come back."

But young Mark observed to his cousin Sammle, "It takes longer, every year, for Grandmother to grow accustomed."

And Sammle said, shivering, though it was warm May weather, "Perhaps one year, when they come back, she will not be here. She is becoming so tiny and thin; you can see right through her hands, as if they were leaves." And Sammle held up her own thin brown young hand against the sunlight, to see the blood glow under the translucent skin.

"I don't know how they would bear it," said Mark thoughtfully, "if when they came back we had to tell them that she had died."

But that was not what happened.

One December the Uncles arrived much later than usual. They did not climb the mountain until St. Mishan's Day, and when they reached the house it was in silence. There was none of the usual joyful commotion.

Grandmother knew instantly that there was something wrong.

"Where is my son Mark?" she demanded. "Why do I not hear him among you?"

And Uncle Acraud had to tell her: "Mother, he is dead. Your son Mark will not come home, ever again."

"How do you *know*? How can you be *sure*? You were not there when he died?"

"I waited and waited at our meeting place, and a messenger came to tell me. His caravan had been attacked by wild tribesmen, riding north from the Lark mountains. Mark was killed, and all his people. Only this one man escaped and came to bring me the story."

"But how can you be *sure*? How do you know he told the *truth*?"

"He brought Mark's ring."

Emer put it into her hand. As she turned it about in her thin fingers, a long moan went through her.

"Yes, he is dead. My son Mark is dead."

"The man gave me this little box," Acraud said, "which Mark was bringing for you."

Emer put it into her hand, opening the box for her. Inside lay an ivory fan. On it, when it was spread out, you could see a bird, with eyes made of sapphire, flying across a valley, but Grandmother held it listlessly, as if her hands were numb.

"What is it?" she said. "I do not know what it is. Help me to bed, Argilla. I do not know what it is. I do not wish to know. My son Mark is dead."

Her grief infected the whole village. It was as if the keystone of an arch had been knocked out; there was nothing to hold the people together.

That year spring came early, and the three remaining Uncles, melancholy and restless, were glad to leave on their travels. Grandmother hardly noticed their going.

Sammle said to Mark: "You are clever with your hands. Could you not make a pipe—like the one my father had?"

"*I?*" he said. "Make a pipe? Like Uncle Mark's pipe? Why? What would be the point of doing so?"

"Perhaps you might learn to play on it. As he did."

"*I?* Play on a pipe?"

"I think you could," she said. "I have heard you whistle tunes of your own."

"But where would I find the right kind of wood?"

"There is a chest, in which Uncle Gonfil once brought books and music from Leiden. I think it is the same kind of wood. I think you could make a pipe from it."

"But how can I remember the shape?"

"I will make a drawing," Sammle said, and she drew with a stick of charcoal on the whitewashed wall of the cowshed. As soon as Mark looked at her drawing he began to contradict.

"No! I remember now. It was not like that. The stops came here—and the mouthpiece was like this."

Now the other children flocked around to help and advise.

"The stops were farther apart," said Creusie. "And there were more of them and they were bigger."

"The pipe was longer than that," said Sandri. "I have held it. It was as long as my arm."

"How will you ever make the stops?" said young Emer.

"You can have my silver bracelets that Father gave me," said Sammle.

"I'll ask Finn the smith to help me," said Mark.

Once he had got the notion of making a pipe into his head, he was eager to begin. But it took him several weeks of difficult carving; the black wood of the chest proved hard as iron. And when the pipe was made, and the stops fitted, it would not play; try as he would, not a note could he fetch out of it.

Mark was dogged, though, once he had set himself to a task; he took another piece of the black chest, and began again. Only Sammle stayed to help him now; the other children had lost hope, or interest, and gone back to their summer occupations.

The second pipe was much better than the first. By September, Mark was able to play a few notes on it; by October he was playing simple tunes, made up out of his head.

"But," he said, "if I am to play so that Grandmother can see with her fingers—if I am to do *that*—I must remember your father's special tune. Can *you* remember it, Sammle?"

She thought and thought.

"Sometimes," she said, "it seems as if it is just beyond the edge of my hearing—as if somebody were playing it, far, far away, in the woods. Oh, if only I could stretch my hearing a little farther!"

"Oh, Sammle! Try!"

For days and days she sat silent, or wandered in the woods, frowning, knotting her forehead, willing her ears to hear the tune again; and the women of the household said, "That girl is not doing her fair share of the tasks."

They scolded her, and set her to spin, weave, milk the goats, throw grain to the hens. But all the while she continued silent, listening, listening, to a sound she could not hear. At night, in her dreams, she sometimes thought she could hear the tune, and she would wake with tears on her cheeks, wordlessly calling her father to come back and play his music to her, so that she could remember it.

In September the autumn winds blew cold and fierce; by October snow was piled around the walls and up to the windowsills. On St. Felin's Day the three Uncles returned, but sadly and silently, without the former festivities; although, as usual, they brought many bales and boxes of gifts and merchandise. The children went down as usual, to help carry the bundles up the mountain. The joy had gone out of this tradition though; they toiled silently up the track with their loads.

It was a wild, windy evening, the sun set in fire, the

wind moaned among the fir trees, and gusts of sleet every now and then dashed in their faces.

"Take care, children!" called Uncle Emer, as they skirted along the side of a deep gully, and his words were caught by an echo and flung back and forth between the rocky walls: "Take care—care—care—care—care—. . ."

"*Oh!*" cried Sammle, stopping precipitately and clutching the bag that she was carrying. "I have it! I can remember it! *Now* I know how it went!"

And, as they stumbled on up the snowy hillside, she hummed the melody to her cousin Mark, who was just ahead of her.

"Yes, that is it, yes!" he said. "Or, no, wait a minute, that is not *quite* right—but it is close, it is very nearly the way it went. Only the notes were a little faster, and there were more of them—they went up, not down—before the ending tied them in a knot—"

"No, no, they went down at the end, I am almost sure. . . ."

Arguing, interrupting each other, disputing, agreeing, they dropped their bundles in the family room and ran away to the cowhouse, where Mark kept his pipe hidden.

For three days they discussed and argued and tried a hundred different versions; they were so occupied that they hardly took the trouble to eat. But at last, by Christmas morning, they had reached agreement.

"I *think* it is right," said Sammle. "And if it is not, I

do not believe there is anything more that we can do about it."

"Perhaps it will not work in any case," said Mark sadly. He was tired out with arguing and practicing.

Sammle was equally tired, but she said, "Oh, it *must* work. Oh, let it work! Please let it work! For otherwise I don't think I can bear the sadness. Go now, Mark, quietly and quickly, go and stand behind Granny's chair."

The family had gathered, according to Christmas habit, around Grandmother's rocking chair, but the faces of the Uncles were glum and reluctant, their wives dejected and hopeless. Only the children showed eagerness, as the cloth-wrapped bundles were brought and laid at Grandmother's feet.

She herself looked wholly dispirited and cast down. When Uncle Emer handed her a slender, soft package, she received it apathetically, almost with dislike, as if she would prefer not to be bothered by this tiresome gift ceremony.

Then Mark, who had slipped through the crowd without being noticed, began to play on his pipe just behind Grandmother's chair.

The Uncles looked angry and scandalized; Aunt Tassy cried out in horror: "Oh, Mark, wicked boy, how *dare* you?" but Grandmother lifted her head, more alertly than she had done for months past, and began to listen.

Mark played on. His mouth was quivering so badly that it was hard to grip the amber mouthpiece, but he played with all the breath that was in him. Meanwhile

Sammle, kneeling by her grandmother, held, with her own warm young hands, the old, brittle ones against the fabric of the gift. And, as she did so, she began to feel what Grandmother felt.

Grandmother said softly and distinctly: "It is a muslin shawl, embroidered in gold thread, from Lebanon. It is colored a soft brick-red, with pale roses of sunset-pink, and thorns of soft silver-green. It is for Sammle. . . ."

The Dog on
the Roof

Not many years ago there was an old lady living in Washington Square, New York. Her name was Mrs. Logan, and she lived right in the park; she hung her clothes on a tree, on coat hangers, and ate her breakfast sitting on a bench. She lived there with her cab-horse, Murphy— and her cab too, of course.

They are not there now. This is the story of why they lived there, and why they left.

At the time I am speaking of, there was also a poet, called Paul Powdermaker, living in a fourth-floor studio in a house in Twelfth Street, five minutes' walk from Washington Square.

Living with Paul was a Labrador dog called Bayer. Bayer was big, with a thick black shiny coat and thoughtful brown eyes. Paul had taken charge of Bayer when his previous owner moved to Patagonia. Paul was not accustomed to dogs, but he had a very kind nature. Bayer was good-natured too, as black Labradors mostly are, and the two got on well. (Poets and dogs nearly always do get on well; they speak the same language.)

Bayer had only one bad habit: of course he did not consider it bad, but some people might. His previous owner had trained him to howl at the sound of a Salvation Army band—or any music played in the street. At the first sound of a transistor, or people singing, or drums, or guitars, Bayer would start to bark and howl and carry on, making as much noise as he could to drown the music.

Paul had one fault too: he never took Bayer out for a walk. He didn't realize that dogs need adventures.

Luckily in the studio they shared there was a door that led out on to the roof. So, five or six times a day, Bayer would pad over to this door and give a short, polite bark; then Paul would get up, pen in hand, open the door, shut it again behind Bayer, and go on with his writing, which he did for twenty hours a day.

Once outside, Bayer would suddenly change from being a rather fat, slow, sleepy, lazy indoor dog to a keen, alert, active (but still rather fat), outdoor one.

First he would rush to the edge of the roof and look down to see what was going on in Twelfth Street. Then he would bark hard, about twenty times, just to announce that he was observing everybody in the street and keeping an eye on everything. There were trees along each side of the street, and birds in them, and sometimes a cat or two in the front gardens, and pigeons and blue jays on the roofs, and a few people strolling or walking briskly.

Sometimes there would be another dog down in the street; then Bayer would bark extra loud. And Bayer had a friend, called Rackstraw, who lived in the basement area of the house along at the corner; so some of his barks were for Rackstraw, and meant, "Good morning! How are you down there? I'm all right up here. Isn't it hot/cold/fine/rainy/frosty/snowy today?"

We shall come back to Rackstraw later.

When Bayer had finished his barking, he would take off like a champion hurdler and race right along the block all the way from one end to the other and then back, several times. The roofs were not all flat. Some sloped up to parapets; some were two or three feet higher than their neighbors; here and there, studio skylights stuck up like big triangular boxes; or there were clusters of chimneys like giants' fingers, or water tanks on legs which looked like pointed rockets about to take off.

Bayer knew all this landscape of roof as well as most dogs know their backyards, and he went bounding along, clearing the walls like a greyhound, nipping among and through the chimneys like a polo pony, skirting around the water tanks and studio skylights like a St. Bernard on the slopes of the Alps. Bayer had a very good head for heights, and, though he often dashed right to the edge of a roof and barked so hard that he looked as if he were going to bark himself right off, he had never done so yet.

When he had breathed in enough fresh air, he would return to his own door, and let out another short polite bark, and Paul Powdermaker would let him in.

Though he worked so hard at it, Paul did not earn a very good living from his poetry writing. Very few poets do. He wrote hundreds of poems, and sent them to dozens of magazines, but hardly any of his poems were printed. And the payment for those that were printed was not high. So, as well as poetry, Paul wrote fortunes for the fortune cookies used in Chinese restaurants. He was paid for this work not in money but in big boxes of free fortune cookies; and these were what he and Bayer mostly ate. Bayer had become very expert at eating the cookies and spitting out the slips of paper with the fortunes printed on them.

One sharp December evening Paul had just let out Bayer, and was writing a fortune for a cookie: "Never hide inside a teapot. Someone might pour boiling water on you." At this moment he heard Bayer up above on the roof, barking much louder than usual.

Paul opened the window, leaned out, and looked down to see what was causing Bayer's agitation.

Down below on the sidewalk, clustered around a little ginkgo tree, he saw a group of carol singers with two guitars and a drum. They were singing "The Holly and the Ivy" and, up above, Bayer was accompanying them by howling as loudly as he could. They weren't a Salvation Army band but, so far as Bayer was concerned, there wasn't a lot of difference. He stood right on the edge of the roof and made a noise like a police siren with hiccups, jerking himself backward and forward with every bark.

The carol singers didn't mind Bayer; they thought he was joining in out of Christmas spirit; in any case he didn't sound so loud to them, four stories down, because they were making a good deal of noise themselves.

In the midst of all this commotion, old Mrs. Logan drove slowly along the street in her horse-drawn cab. Mrs. Logan was not really driving the cab; she was asleep. Her horse, Murphy, knew the way home perfectly well. So Mrs. Logan was inside the cab, having a nap, while Murphy plodded thoughtfully along, taking his time. They were returning from their usual day's inactivity, spent outside a big hotel, the Plaza, waiting for customers who might wish to drive around Central Park or along the main shopping streets in an open horse-drawn cab. Very few customers *did* want to at such a cold time of year. And if by any chance they felt like a cab ride, they hardly ever picked Mrs. Logan's cab, because Murphy, a brown horse the color of gingerbread, was so terribly thin that his ribs resembled a rusty radiator; they looked as if you could play a tune by running a stick across them. Murphy looked as if his maximum speed would be about half a mile per hour.

So customers generally picked cabs with fatter, stronger horses. And tonight, as on nearly all other evenings, Murphy and Mrs. Logan were coming home to their sleeping quarters in Washington Square without having had a single fare all day. Mrs. Logan would then wrap Murphy in a lot of old quilts she kept folded up in a cardboard box; and she would wrap herself up in a lot more; and they would share a supper of half-eaten rolls, ends of pretzels, bits of sandwiches, and other food that Mrs. Logan had picked out of garbage cans early that morning. Then they would go to sleep, Murphy standing, Mrs. Logan sleeping in the cab, which would be parked under a big stone arch, the Washington Arch.

No policeman ever bothered Mrs. Logan.

The first time she spent a night in Washington Square a policeman called O'Grady said to her, "Ma'am, you shouldn't be camping here, you know."

"Ah, now, have a heart, dear boy," said Mrs. Logan. "I'm from way back in the country, from the lovely little town of Four Corners, New Hampshire—and the sight of the green leaves and the squirrels in this park will be easing the sadness of my poor homesick heart. I tell you what, Officer O'Grady," she said, "I'll be singing you a song now."

So she sang him a beautiful song that went:

> When an Irish Robin
> Hops into your waistcoat pocket
> Won't your ould heart shoot up
> Like a fine skyrocket?
> Remember the nest
> In the Isle of the Blest
> With four beautiful eggs of blue
> Where an Irish Robin
> Is waiting and singing
> For you!

Officer O'Grady was so charmed by this song, which Mrs. Logan sang in a very sweet voice, thin as a thread but dead on the note, that he immediately gave her leave to stay under the Washington Arch just as long as she liked, and furthermore he told all his friends in the Sixth Precinct office that Mrs. Logan was not to be bothered.

So all that any of the other policemen did was to pass the time of day and keep a friendly eye on her, and sometimes ask her to sing the song about the Irish Robin, which she always did for them.

Just as Mrs. Logan and Murphy drew abreast of the carol singers (who had now got to "The First Noel"), Bayer, up above on the roof, became so overexcited that he did something he never had before: he barked himself right off the roof, and fell like a heavy black plum, down, down, four stories, until, as luck would have it (and very fortunately), he landed on the canvas hood of Mrs. Logan's cab. This worked as well as a trampoline; Bayer bounced on it a couple of times, then he tumbled into the cab itself, not hurt at all, but a trifle surprised.

Mrs. Logan was surprised too.

"Musha!" she said. "Will ye be believing it now, dogs falling from the sky! What next, at all?"

Bayer politely removed himself from the cab, and jumped to the ground.

"Are you hurt?" inquired Murphy, who was just as surprised as Mrs. Logan, but not given to exclaiming.

"No, thank you, not at all," said Bayer. "I hope I didn't frighten your driver."

"Oh, very little frightens Mrs. Logan. She is quite a calm person," said Murphy, and he went on plodding in the direction of Washington Square.

Bayer felt that, now he was down in the street, he might as well take advantage of the opportunity. It was a long time since he had had the chance to run about and sniff all the delicious smells at ground level, and he was fairly sure that Paul would not begin to worry about him for some time. So he loped along companionably beside Murphy, slowing his pace to the horse's tired, stumbling walk.

When the cab came to a stop under the Washington Arch, and Mrs. Logan wrapped up herself and the horse, and divided a handful of crusts and pretzel-ends between them, Bayer was rather shocked.

"Don't you have a proper stable?" he asked the horse. "And is that *all* you get for supper?"

Compared with this, Bayer's own quarters in the fourth-floor studio and his supper of fortune cookies seemed comfortable, even princely.

"How long have you lived here?" he asked.

"Nine or ten years, I suppose," said Murphy.

"Can't you find anything better?"

"Mrs. Logan hasn't any money," Murphy explained, and then he told the story of how they came to be living under the Washington Arch.

"We come from a little town many hundreds of miles from here," he said, heaving a sigh that went all along his bony ribs, like a finger along the keys of a piano. "It is called Four Corners, New Hampshire, and there *are* only four corners in it—and the train station of course. We used to wait at the station, and as ours was the only cab, we made a good living. Mrs. Logan lived with her brother, who has a farm. But one day four men got off the train and asked if we would take them all the way to New York. They offered eighty dollars for the ride. I've begun to think, lately, that perhaps they were robbers. On the way down (which took several days) they talked a lot about banks, and money, and the police.

"When we reached New York they said they hadn't any cash on them, but if Mrs. Logan would be outside the Plaza Hotel next morning at ten, they would be there to pay her the eighty dollars. So we spent the night here and went to the Plaza next day; but the men never turned up with the money. And, though we have gone back there each morning at ten ever since, we have never seen them again."

"What a set of scoundrels!" exclaimed Bayer. "Maybe they never meant to pay you at all."

"That is what I begin to think," agreed Murphy sadly. "But Mrs. Logan still believes they will turn up one of these days; she thinks they must be having a little difficulty earning the money."

"Why don't you both go back to Four Corners?"

"Oh, Mrs. Logan would never do that. She would think that looked as if she didn't trust the men to keep their promise. But," said Murphy, sighing again, "I am growing very tired of the city—though it is so grand—I

often wish I was back in my own stable at Four Corners—
especially on a cold night like this one."

That night was bitterly cold; the stars shone bright as
flares, and the moon was big as an ice rink. Far away
along Fifth Avenue the pointed tower of the Empire State
Building glowed pink and green and blue against the night
sky. All the squirrels of Washington Square were curled
up tight in their nests; the rollerskaters and skateboarders
and the Frisbee-slingers had long gone home to bed. Mrs.
Logan and Murphy and Bayer were the only live creatures there, standing patiently under the Washington
Arch.

"Well, *I* think it's a shocking shame," said Bayer, and
then he trotted away, thinking hard as he went. He was
going home, but first he intended to consult another
acquaintance of his who lived in the basement area at
the end of Twelfth Street.

This was a skunk named Rackstraw. Bayer and Rackstraw often held conversations, from roof to street, but
up till now they had never met face to face.

Rackstraw had not been in Twelfth Street very long.
He had arrived one day in a Rolls Royce car; Bayer wanted
to know more about him.

The basement area of the end house held several trash
cans, a box or two, a stone trough containing laurel
bushes, and a Styrofoam picnic basket lined with newspaper.

The carolers were now singing "Good King Wenceslas"
at the other end of the block, so Bayer went, a little warily,

down a couple of the stone steps that led to the basement door, and called, loud enough for the skunk to hear over the music, "Rackstraw? Are you at home?"

Instantly Rackstraw's handsome black and white head poked out of the picnic basket.

"Good heavens, Bayer! Is that you? What in the world are you doing down in the street?"

"Oh, I just jumped down," Bayer said carelessly. "There was no problem about it, I landed on the roof of Mrs. Logan's cab."

"My stars! I wouldn't dare do a thing like that!" said Rackstraw. He spoke with an English accent. Bayer had noticed this before; he recognized the English accent because Paul Powdermaker had an English friend called Lord Donisthorpe.

"Do you come from England?" Bayer inquired. "I didn't know there were English skunks."

"I was born and brought up in an English zoo," explained Rackstraw. "But my mother always told me that I ought to return to the land of my ancestors, if I could. The zoo where I lived was in a large park, where there were a lot of other entertainments as well—outdoor plays, and opera, and circuses. Last month an opera was being performed, and the audience ate picnic suppers by their cars in between the acts. I was hidden in a bush munching a piece of smoked salmon I had managed to pick up when I heard American voices. Somebody said, 'We'll drive the car on board the ship tomorrow.' I thought, Now's my chance! So, while they were eating, I climbed into the luggage compartment of their car (which was a Rolls Royce) and hid under a rug. The next day the car was driven onto a ship, which sailed to New York. The trip took five days."

"And you were in the luggage place all that time?" Bayer was greatly impressed. "Didn't you run out of air and food?"

"There was plenty to eat, because they had left the remains of the picnic—bread and cheese and salmon and fruit and salad and plum cake. And the trunk was a big airy place. When we reached New York and they drove away from the dock I waited for my chance, and as soon as they opened the lid of the trunk I shot out. This was where they stopped, on Twelfth Street, so I have lived here ever since. It isn't bad—the people in the house are quite kind and give me fried potatoes; but in the spring I shall move on."

"Where to?"

"Back to the place my mother and father came from. There are some cousins still living there. It is Mount Mosscrop, a hill in New Hampshire near a little town called Four Corners."

"Why!" exclaimed Bayer, amazed, "that's where Murphy comes from!" and then he told Rackstraw the story of Mrs. Logan.

Rackstraw said thoughtfully, "If only we could persuade Mrs. Logan to go back home, I could ride with her as a passenger."

"You could if you promised—"

"Promised what?"

All this time, Bayer had been keeping at a careful distance from his neighbor. Now he said, rather hesitantly, "Well—er—I was brought up in the city, I never met a skunk before, personally, that is. But, well, I always heard—I was told that skunks—that you were able to—that is to say—"

"Oh," said Rackstraw, "you mean the smell?"

"Well—yes," apologized Bayer, moving back onto a higher step, lest the skunk had taken offense. But Rackstraw did not seem annoyed.

"My mother trained me not to, except in emergencies," he said. "People in England are very polite; they don't like it. And my mother was very particular about manners. 'Never, never do it,' she used to say, 'unless you are in great danger.' So I never have."

"It never happens by accident?"

"I suppose it might—if one were to sneeze violently— but it never has to me. Now, let's think how we can persuade Mrs. Logan to return to Four Corners."

Just then they heard the voice of Paul Powdermaker, who was walking slowly along the street, whistling and calling: "Bayer? Bayer? Where are you?"

"We'll talk about this again," said Bayer hastily. "It's good to have met you. See you soon. Take care!"

"Good night!" called Rackstraw, and he slipped back into his cozy, insulated nest.

Bayer ran along Twelfth Street with his master, and climbed the seventy-four stairs back to their warm studio, where he had a late-night snack of fortune cookies. One of them said: "A bone contains much that is noble. And L is for love."

"Did you write that?" Bayer said to Paul. "I don't think much of it."

"One can't hit top notes all the time," said Paul, who was hard at work on a long poem about the ocean. "Don't distract me now, there's a dear fellow. And, next time you want to go into the street, warn me in advance; I nearly dropped dead of fright when I saw you jump off the roof."

Bayer apologized for causing Paul so much anxiety, and climbed into his basket. But it was a long time before he slept. He kept thinking of Mrs. Logan and Murphy, out in the bitter cold, under the Washington Arch, waiting for morning to come.

After that day, Bayer always kept his ears pricked for the sound of Murphy's hoofs slowly clopping along the street. When he heard them, he would bark to go out on the roof. Mrs. Logan formed the habit of putting up the hood of her cab when she drove along Twelfth Street, and Bayer would jump down onto the hood, bounce once or twice, and then either ride on the box with Mrs. Logan, or run in the street beside Murphy. Paul grew accustomed to this, and stopped worrying. Bayer made himself useful helping Mrs. Logan hunt for edible tidbits in trash cans— he was much better at it than the old lady—and he spent many days in town with the pair, talking to Murphy and keeping an eye out for the four men who owed Mrs. Logan eighty dollars.

"One of them was tall and thin, with glasses," Murphy told Bayer, "one was little and round with a red nose; one was very pale, white-haired and blue-eyed; and one was dotted all over with freckles and had red hair. They rode with us for so many days that I had plenty of time to get to know them."

Mrs. Logan's cab was parked outside the Plaza Hotel. She nodded sleepily in the sunshine, while Bayer and Murphy watched all the well-dressed people pass by. As Christmas was near, there were several men dressed as Santa Claus, ringing bells and collecting money for charity. Whenever they rang their bells, Bayer barked, but not so loudly as he would have three weeks ago; these days, Bayer didn't bark so loudly or so often, and since he was getting more exercise, he was not so fat.

He found a chunk of pretzel in the gutter and offered it to Murphy.

"How about you?" said the horse. "Wouldn't you like it?"

"Oh, I'll be getting my fortune cookies later on."

"Well—thanks, then."

"What's your favorite food?" Bayer asked, as Murphy hungrily chewed the pretzel.

"Spinach," answered Murphy when he had swallowed. "Mrs. Logan always buys me a bag of spinach if we earn any money. Up at Four Corners," he said sighing, "I used to be given as much spinach as I could eat; I had bushels of it. Mrs. Logan's brother grew fields and fields of it, and I used to do the plowing for him."

"*Spinach?*" cried Bayer. "I never heard of anybody liking *that* stuff!"

That evening, when Bayer was back at home, he sat beside Paul and laid a paw beseechingly on the poet's knee.

Paul wrote:

> The ocean, like a great eye
> Stares at the sky.

Then he stopped writing and stared at the dog.

"What's the trouble, Bayer? Do you want another fortune cookie?"

"No," said Bayer, "I need a whole lot of spinach."

"*Spinach!*" exclaimed Paul, just as Bayer had earlier. "What do you need that for?"

"For a friend."

"Spinach—spinach—" Paul began to mumble, coming out of his poem slowly like a mouse out of a cheese. "Now let me think—I read something about spinach in the paper—two or three days ago it was—"

Paul had *The New York Times* delivered every day, and there were piles of newspapers lying about all over the floor. He rummaged around in these untidy heaps, and it took ever so long before he found what he wanted.

" '*Load of Spinach Goes Begging,*' " he read aloud to Bayer. " 'A freighter packed to the portholes with spinach is lying at anchor off the Morton Street pier, waiting for

81

somebody to buy up her load. The asking price is twenty dollars. The ship met with such severe gales on the way to New York from Florida that the usual two-day run was extended to eight. Consequently the cargo has deteriorated, and New York greengrocers are not keen to buy. The owner will probably accept a giveaway price if anyone is prepared to take his load off his hands. Come along, Popeye, here's your chance!' "

"*Twenty dollars*," thought Bayer sadly. "That's a terrible lot of money. But a whole load of spinach would certainly set Murphy on his feet again, and make him fit for the trip back to Four Corners."

The next day at seven, Bayer was out on the roof although it was still dark and bitterly cold. The streetlamps down below glimmered like Christmas oranges in the bare trees of Twelfth Street. Bayer heard the slow clip-clop of Murphy's hoofs coming along, and he jumped down as usual, bouncing lightly off the canvas hood onto the road below. He trotted beside the cab, and was about to tell Murphy of the boatload of spinach off the Morton Street pier when a most unexpected thing happened.

Around the corner of the street marched fifty-seven Santa Clauses.

They were wearing Father Christmas costumes. Some carried sacks, and some had bells. Many held Christmas trees. They marched in rows: five rows of ten, and one row of seven.

Mrs. Logan, who had been dozing on the box, woke up and stared with astonishment at the sight.

"Glory be to goodness!" she murmured. "That's enough Santa Clauses for every week in the year, so it is, and five more for luck!"

Then she looked more closely at the last row of Santa Clauses, who were breaking rank to pass the cab, and she cried out, "Divil fly away with me if those aren't the fellas that rode with us down from Four Corners, New Hampshire! Will ye be after giving me my eighty dollars now, if ye please?" she called to them.

Murphy recognized the men at the same instant, and he whinnied loudly; Bayer, catching the general excitement, barked his head off. Rackstraw bounced out of his nest.

Most of the Father Christmases seemed mildly surprised at this; but four of them dropped their Christmas trees and bolted away, as if they had suddenly remembered they had a train to catch.

Murphy did his best to chase them; but he was far too thin and tired to keep up more than a very slow canter for a couple of blocks, and the men easily got away from him; very soon they were out of sight. Bayer and Rackstraw followed a few blocks farther, but they, too, lost the men in the end. One of the men, however, had dropped a wallet in his fright; Bayer pounced on that and carried it back in triumph. Inside were four five-dollar bills. Twenty dollars!

The owner of the freighter anchored off the Morton Street pier was greatly astonished when a shabby old cab, drawn by a skeleton-thin old horse, drew up on the dock by his ship, and an old lady, waving a handful of green paper money, offered to buy his load.

"Certainly you can have it," the owner said. "But where will you put it? The Port Authority won't allow you to leave it on the dock."

"Ah, sure, then, they'll let me keep it there for a night or so," said Mrs. Logan hopefully. "And in the meanwhile old Murphy here will eat a great, great deal of it."

So the load of spinach was dumped out on the dock. It was in a very limp and wilted state, but even so it made a massive pile, twenty feet high and thirty feet long. Murphy gazed as if, even now he saw it, he could hardly believe his eyes.

"Go on then, ye poor ould quadruped," said Mrs. Logan. "Eat your head off, for once."

Murphy didn't wait to be told twice. After ten minutes he had made a hole as big as himself in the green mountain of spinach. Then Mrs. Logan packed as much spinach as she could into the cab.

Murphy reluctantly stopped eating—"Best ye don't gobble too much all at once," Mrs. Logan warned him, "or 'tis desperate heartburn ye'll be getting—" and they started slowly back toward Washington Square.

Lifting the spinach and packing it into the cab had been a hard, heavy job, and it made a heavy load to pull; Bayer could see that Mrs. Logan and Murphy were not going to be able to shift very many loads before nightfall. And a Port Authority inspector was walking up and down, looking disapprovingly at the hill of spinach.

Bayer galloped back to Twelfth Street to consult with Rackstraw.

Greatly to his surprise, when he reached the door of his own house, he saw, parked at the curb, the very same white Rolls Royce that had brought Rackstraw to the city. And on the doorstep Paul Powdermaker was enthusiastically shaking the hand of his English friend, Lord Donisthorpe.

"Oh, please, oh, please, Paul, dear Paul, we need your help and advice very badly!" exclaimed Bayer, bounding all around Paul in his agitation.

Lord Donisthorpe, who was a thin elderly English gentleman with a tuft of gray hair like a secretary-bird and a long nose, and a pair of spectacles which were always halfway down it, gazed with a mild dreamy interest at Bayer. Lord Donisthorpe knew a great deal about animals; in fact he was the owner of the zoo from which Rackstraw had escaped.

"Gracious me, my dear Paul! How very remarkable and touching! You and the dog are in verbal communication! You talk to one another! That is remarkably interesting. I shall certainly write a paper on it, for the Royal Society."

"Oh, it's nothing," said Paul, rather shyly and shortly. "Poets and dogs generally understand one another, I believe. Well, Bayer, what is it? Can't whatever it is wait for a few minutes? Lord Donisthorpe has just arrived from his Mexican trip—"

85

"Oh, no, Paul, it can't, you see it's that mountain of spinach by the Morton Street pier that Mrs. Logan wants to move to Washington Square—the spinach has to be moved today or the Port Authority will tell the sanitation trucks to take it away. But we need a car or a truck—Mrs. Logan and Murphy can't possibly manage it all on their own."

Paul—whose mind was still half on his ocean poem—could not make head or tail of this at first, and it needed endless repetitions before he managed to understand what Bayer was talking about. By that time Lord Donisthorpe had also grasped the nature of the problem; and the sight of Murphy and Mrs. Logan doggedly plodding along Twelfth Street with another load of spinach finally brought it home to both men.

Lord Donisthorpe ran out into the street and took hold of Murphy's bridle. Murphy came to a relieved stop.

"My dear ma'am! Excuse me—ahem!—I am not usually one to meddle in other people's affairs—but I own a zoo, in England—I do know quite a lot about animals—and that horse, my dear ma'am—really that horse is too thin to be pulling a cab so laden with spinach. What he needs, if you will forgive my saying so, is about twenty square meals."

"Man, dear, don't I know it!" said Mrs. Logan. "And there's about a hundred square meals waiting for the blessed crayture; if only we can get the stuff shifted to Washington Square."

———

The end of it was that Paul Powdermaker and Lord Donisthorpe spent the rest of the day shifting spinach from the dockside to Washington Square in Lord Donisthorpe's Rolls. They had just delivered the last load before darkness fell. In the middle of Washington Square there is a paved area; all the spinach was piled here in a huge mound, the height and shape of an outsize Christmas tree.

Mrs. Logan and Murphy passed the day resting; Mrs. Logan thought long and hard, while Murphy ate. Bayer ran back and forth alongside the Rolls, and greatly enjoyed himself.

Police Officer O'Grady had long ago been moved on from that precinct; but another policeman called O'Brien walked by at dusk and thoughtfully surveyed the huge pile of spinach.

"I doubt ye won't be allowed to keep that there, ma'am," he said mildly.

"Ah, glory be! Where else can I keep it, at all?" said Mrs. Logan.

"Well, maybe it can stay there till just after Christmas," said O'Brien.

"In that case there's no call to worry; Murphy will have ate it all by then."

Indeed, during the next few days Murphy munched so diligently at the great pile that it shrank and shrank, first to the size of an upended bus; then to the size of Lord Donisthorpe's car; and finally to no size at all. Meanwhile, Murphy, from all this good nourishing food, grew bigger and bigger; his coat became thick and glossy; his head, which had hung down like a wet sock, reared up proudly; his mane and tail grew three inches a day, and even his hoofs began to shine. He took to trotting, and then to cantering, around and around Washington Square, among the rollerskaters; he even frisked a little, and kicked up his heels.

During this time Lord Donisthorpe and Paul Powder-maker had many conversations with Mrs. Logan over cups of tea and muffins in a coffee shop in University Place.

"If I were you, ma'am," said Lord Donisthorpe, "I would wait no longer, hoping to get your money back. I fear those wretches who deceived you are gone for good. If I were you, I should take that fine horse of yours, and go back to Four Corners, New Hampshire."

Mrs. Logan needed a lot of convincing. But in the end she did agree. "Isn't it a sad thing there should be so much wickedness in the heart of man?" she said. "'Tis the city folk that are bad, I'm thinking. True enough, I'll be glad to go back to Four Corners."

"What will you do for food along the way?" said Paul. "It's not so easy to pick up broken pretzels and sandwich crusts in the country."

Mrs. Logan had an idea about that.

"Now Murphy's in such grand shape, I reckon we'll be entering for the Christmas Day cab-horse race. If we win, 'tis a five-hundred-dollar prize; that money would buy us journey food back to Four Corners, and leave plenty over a Christmas gift for my brother Sean, who must have thought me dead these ten years."

"Christmas race?" said Lord Donisthorpe. "If Murphy wins that—and I really don't see why he should not—it will be a fine endorsement for my Spinach Diet Plan for horses. I shall write a paper about it for the Royal Society. . . ."

So it was agreed that Murphy and Mrs. Logan should enter for the race.

Paul and Lord Donisthorpe polished up the cab, and the brass bits of Murphy's harness, checked the reins, saddle soaped the leather, and waxed the woodwork, until the cab looked—not new, but a bit better than it had before. And they tied a big red rosette on Murphy's headband.

But meanwhile there was trouble brewing in Twelfth Street.

At this time of year, people had naturally been buying Christmas trees and taking them home, putting them in pots and decorating them with tinsel and lights.

But after a couple of days in warm houses, many of the trees began to smell truly terrible.

A meeting of the Twelfth Street Block Association was held.

"It's that skunk living at the end of the street!" people said. "We always knew that having a skunk in the street would lead to trouble. That skunk has to go."

Paul Powdermaker argued that this was unfair and

unreasonable. "That skunk—whose name is Rackstraw, I might inform you—has never been near any of your Christmas trees. He has not touched them. How could he? He lives outside in his picnic basket; the trees are inside. There has been no connection. Furthermore he is a very well-behaved skunk; my dog—who ought to know—informs me that Rackstraw never gives offense, in any possible way."

But just the same, the Block Association decided that Rackstraw must be removed to the Central Park Zoo.

Only, nobody quite knew how to set about this. Whose job is it to remove a skunk? First they called the Sanitation Department and asked them to send a garbage truck. The Sanitation Department said it was no business of theirs. The police said the same thing.

The Central Park Zoo said that they would take Rackstraw, if somebody would deliver him; but they were not prepared to come and fetch him.

"You had better stay in my studio till all this blows over," Paul said to Rackstraw. But Rackstraw said that he was not used to living indoors; he would prefer to spend a few days with Mrs. Logan in her cab. So that is what he did.

On Christmas Day large crowds assembled in Central Park to watch the cab race.

For this event the cabs had to race three times all around the park—a distance of eighteen miles. During the morning no traffic was allowed on the streets alongside the park.

All the contestants lined up outside the Plaza Hotel— there were thirty of them, cabs polished to a brilliant dazzle, and gay with ribbons, tinsel, and holly. The horses were in tiptop condition, bouncing and eager to be off. Mrs. Logan's cab was certainly not the smartest; but no horse looked in better shape than Murphy. His coat gleamed like a newly baked bun; and he was snorting with excitement.

Lord Donisthorpe was staying with the friends with whom he had crossed the Atlantic. They lived in a top-floor apartment overlooking the park, so after he and Paul had wished Mrs. Logan well, they went up to the penthouse garden, where they would have a grandstand view of the whole race.

The starter's gun cracked, and, after a couple of false starts, the competitors clattered off, whips cracking and wheels flashing.

During the first lap, Murphy drew so far ahead of all the others that it hardly seemed like a race at all. Galloping like a Derby winner, with Bayer racing at his side barking ecstatically, he tore up Central Park West, turned east along 110th Street, crossed the north end of the park, and came racing down Fifth Avenue. All the other contestants were at least half a mile behind.

Then, as Murphy approached the Plaza Hotel, ready to turn the corner and begin his second lap, something unexpected happened. There were four men in Santa Claus costumes outside the Plaza, and, as Murphy came racing along, he had a clear view of their faces. With a loud neigh of recognition, he swung off the racecourse, and started chasing the men, who fled down Fifth Avenue with Murphy thundering after them.

"What's got into that horse?" yelled the crowd of watchers. "Has he lost his way? Has he gone mad? Murphy, Murphy, you took a wrong turn!"

Mrs. Logan had also spotted the men in Santa Claus costumes and she was shouting, "Musha, wisha, come back, ye spalpeens! What about my sixty dollars?"

(As they had spent the twenty dollars from the wallet on spinach, she reckoned that the men owed her only sixty.)

Before, the men had easily escaped from Murphy. But now they hadn't a chance. Mrs. Logan leaned out with her whip and her umbrella, and hooked them into her cab one by one—helped by enthusiastic people along Fifth Avenue.

Just outside the Forty-Second Street library she grabbed the last Santa Claus. The stone lions in front of the library were roaring their heads off, because it was Christmas; and Murphy whinnied joyfully; and Bayer barked his loudest.

Rackstraw, curled up in the back of the cab, had been rather startled when the thieves were hauled in. For a moment, indeed, he felt tempted to disobey his mother's rule. But he restrained himself. "Politeness always pays, Rackstraw," he remembered his mother saying. So he contented himself with biting the swindlers, who seemed to him to have a terrible smell already.

"Now I have the lot of ye!" said Mrs. Logan. "And it's over to the polis I shall be handing ye, for now I see that ye were a lot of promise-breaking raskills who niver intended to pay me back at all."

By now the police had arrived with sirens screeching and were grouped around the cab waiting to handcuff the Father Christmases. It seemed they had reasons of their own for wanting these men.

So, although Mrs. Logan and Murphy didn't win the Central Park cab race, they did earn the gratitude of the State of New Jersey.

Why? Because these men were Christmas tree thieves, who had been cutting down cedars and spruces along the scenic parkways of New Jersey. But the evergreens had been sprayed by the Highways Department with deer-repellant chemicals, which, when the trees were taken into a warm room, began to smell far, far worse than any skunk. So the stolen trees—and the men who had taken them—were easily identified.

And the grateful Highways Department paid Mrs. Logan a handsome reward.

"I knew the smell of the trees had nothing to do with Rackstraw!" said Bayer.

Rackstraw looked very prim. "I never disobey my mother's rule," he said.

The friends were all back in Washington Square, helping Mrs. Logan and Murphy prepare for their journey.

The cab was stuffed with spinach and pretzels, fried

93

potatoes for Rackstraw, and bottles of root beer for Mrs. Logan.

"How about coming along?" said Murphy to Bayer.

Bayer was deeply tempted. But he said, "I can't leave Paul. He has been very kind to me, and he might be lonely, all on his own."

But inside him Bayer thought sadly how much he would miss his three friends. Poets are poor company, even if they do understand dog language.

"Good-bye, then," said Murphy.

"Good-bye! Good-bye!" called Rackstraw and Mrs. Logan. All Mrs. Logan's police friends had come to the square to wave her good-bye—and a big crowd of other people as well. Newspaper cameras flashed. It was a grand send-off. Mrs. Logan sang her Irish Robin song for the last time; then they started.

As Bayer watched the cab roll away, a huge lump swelled up in his throat. In a moment he knew that a terrible anguished howl was going to come out.

Just then Paul Powdermaker pushed his way through the crowd.

"Bayer," he said, "Lord Donisthorpe has invited me to travel to England and spend a year in his castle. I'd like to go—but if I take you, it means you will have to spend six months in quarantine kennels. The English are very strict about that. So I was wondering if you'd care to go to New Hampshire with Mrs. Logan and Murphy—?"

Bayer turned his head and saw that the cab was out of sight. Murphy had broken into a gallop and was whirling

Mrs. Logan out of New York faster than any crack stage-coach.

"I'd never catch up with them now," said Bayer.

"Nonsense, my dear dog!" exclaimed Lord Donis-thorpe. "What's a Rolls for, may I ask? A good goer Murphy may be, but I never yet heard of a horse who could outrun a Rolls Royce. . . . Jump in, and we'll soon be up with them."

Bayer and Paul leaped into the white Rolls—which still had a certain amount of spinach clinging to its gray tweed upholstery—the motor came to life with a soft purr, and the great car lifted away like a helicopter.

Just the same, Murphy had gone forty miles before they caught up with him.

So that is why, if you go to Washington Square, New York, you won't find Mrs. Logan hanging her dresses on a tree and singing about the Irish Robin, or Murphy the horse standing under the Washington Arch. They are back in Four Corners, New Hampshire, and Bayer the Labrador and Rackstraw the skunk are with them.

The Missing Heir

In the ancient region of London that is known as Rumbury Town, there is a long, narrow street with the name of Robin's Rents. What does this name mean? Who knows? The street has been a highway for hundreds of years. It leads from the docks and quays by the old Rumbury Canal, south-eastward toward the great black bulk of All Hallows Church. The buildings on either side of the road are high and old, with many stories, pointed roofs, and small windows. Dark alleys lie between them, and their doors often lead directly on to flights of stairs climbing upward into murky wells. Many Londoners never have occasion to go near Robin's Rents in the whole of their lives. It is the kind of street you visit if you wish to buy a hundred engraved visiting cards, or a pocket orrery, or a spindle for a hundred-year-old sewing machine, or a pound of tailor's chalk; old-fashioned shops are found here, tailors and printers and cobblers and mantua makers. In the old days, too, there used to be dozens of bookshops all along the street, dealing in both new and second-hand books. There were stalls outside on the pavement filled with grit-covered volumes at one penny and twopence. Now there are not so many. Rents have grown too high.

At the time of which I speak there were bookshops on the upper floors also: dozens of rooms filled with books were to be found up those steep flights of stone stairs, and learned old men in the rooms sitting quietly among the books, guardians of their dusty treasures.

One spring evening, when the last of winter could still be felt in the air, but when the first swallows could be heard overhead, keening and wheeling over the pointed gables in the green-and-lavender sunset sky, a boy called Dominic was walking leisurely homeward from the printer's shop where he worked as an apprentice, when he saw an elderly blind man waiting to cross the street.

The blind man had silvery-gray hair, and wore dark green glasses, and carried a white stick; Dominic remembered noticing him several times before in the neighborhood.

That evening the traffic was particularly heavy: trucks and wagons and buses and coaches roared and ground and thundered past in a continual stream, and the blind man, who carried a bundle of kindling under one arm and a newspaper and a bag of groceries under the other, seemed reluctant to take his life in his hands and venture into the street; in fact, Dominic did not see how he was ever going to get to the other side. He looked this way, he looked that way; he seemed to listen sharply, cocking his head sideways; but there came no gap in the steady roar of the vehicles.

"Shall I help you, sir?" said Dominic, who was a kind-hearted boy, and in no particular haste to get home; and he touched the elderly man gently on the arm, in case he was deaf as well as blind. Dominic spoke loudly and clearly, so as to make himself heard above the rattle of the traffic; and the man turned his head with an alert movement, like that of a pecking pigeon. Indeed he reminded Dominic in several ways of a pigeon: he was neat and plump, not very tall, with a round face, a beaky nose, and hair just that smooth slate-gray color of a pigeon's wing.

"Thank you, my boy," he said, and Dominic wondered how he was so certain that his helper was a boy. "The traffic along this thoroughfare grows heavier each day, I do believe. Only those with winged heels can dare to cross. I should be glad of your help, for it grows late, and my cat Nero will be growing anxious about me."

"Let me carry the kindling, sir," said Dominic. The bundle was tied with a cord, so he tucked his fingers under the cord, and his other hand through the elder man's free arm.

"There's a gap coming in a couple of minutes, sir," he announced presently, "if you can step nimble."

"Nimble I can step," said the gray-haired man. "It is only my eyes that have betrayed me." And indeed, when Dominic said, "Now, sir!" and urged him forward, he came across neatly and surely between the roaring surges of traffic.

"Bravo!" said the blind man when they reached the farther bank—for it did indeed feel as if they had managed to cross some great thundering waterway dry shod. "I am sure that Moses did no better when he led his followers through the Red Sea. Now let us introduce ourselves. My name is Gideon Murney."

"I am Dominic Toole, sir. I have seen your name somewhere, Mr. Murney."

"Doubtless you have, my boy. Halfway along the street."

Then Dominic recollected a gilt-painted sign: *Gideon Murney, Rare Books*, which hung and swung from a first-floor window, over a die-stamp and lettering shop.

"Will I carry your kindling home for you, Mr. Murney?" he suggested. "It's a fair step along the street from here, and this is a heavy old bundle."

"Thank you, Dominic. I'll not say no. It *is* a fair step along the street, and a fair step up the stairs."

Now they were safe on the pavement, however, Mr. Murney walked along confidently, like a man who has trodden this way for the last thirty years, and knows each crack of every paving-stone. They had to pass several bookstores along the way, with trays of volumes still set outside, in hopes of enticing homegoing customers; and at one of these Mr. Murney stopped, and ran his hand over the dusty spines of the books, like a musician fingering an accustomed keyboard.

"Ah!" he said, pausing with his hand on a thick old

brown book that seemed to be bound in crocodile skin. "Gray has not sold his Milton yet, I see. Read me those first lines, my boy, will you, just here—not the prose, where it is set square on the page, but the poetry that runs down like a ribbon."

"Yes, sir? If you wish it?" said Dominic, rather puzzled, and, taking the dusty book from Mr. Murney, he began to read aloud:

"Of man's first disobedience, and the fruit
Of that forbidden tree, whose mortal taste . . .
"Shall I go on, sir?"

"Yes, yes, my boy, just go on reading until I tell you to stop!"

So Dominic continued reading:

"Brought death into the world, and all our woe . . ."
until be arrived at the lines:

"I may assert Eternal Providence,
And justify the ways of God to men."

"Thank you, Dominic, I am very greatly obliged to you," said Mr. Murney at that point. "You have an excellent clear reading voice. I could hear you distinctly, even above the traffic. Now let us be on our way, for I fear that my cat Nero will be becoming deeply agitated."

They walked on until they were directly below the swinging sign that said *Gideon Murney, Rare Books.* A door beside the die-stamp shop opened inward onto a flight of stone stairs.

"I will lead the way," said Mr. Murney, as he climbed briskly to the first floor, where he pulled out a key and opened a door.

The place inside seemed at first to Dominic more like a cave than a room, so piled was it with great ramparts of books—not only in the shelves that lined the walls to the ceiling, but also in barriers across the middle of the floor, so that the space was divided into a number of smaller cell-like compartments. Through and among these Mr. Murney threaded his way with great skill, like a badger returning to its burrow, dislodging not a single volume. Dominic followed him, much more cautiously, to the back of the long room, where there was a window, and a table under it, and a small fireplace framed in books, and a heavy lopsided old swivel armchair, and a shelf of pots and pans, and a narrow bed with a blanket on it. The rays of the setting sun came peacefully through the widow and on to the table. An empty white enamel pie-dish stood on the floor beside the fireplace. But Dominic had eyes for one thing only—the enormous black cat, by far the biggest cat he had ever seen in his entire life, which lay stretched out in luxury across the small table, covering its top completely, enjoying the last warmth of the sun.

"Well, old Nero?" said Mr. Murney. "Were you wondering where I had got to? Did you grow anxious about your master?"

Dominic could detect no signs at all of anxiety in the cat's indolent attitude. But the instant that Mr. Murney pulled a paper-wrapped packet from his bag of groceries, Nero shot down from the table in a flash, and began rubbing himself about his master's legs, purring loudly enough to drown the sound of the distant traffic, and letting out short famished cries, as if he had not been fed for a month.

Mr. Murney unwrapped a good-sized herring, cut it in two, and placed half on the enamel pie-dish; the cat Nero flung himself ravenously on the fish, and had it demolished and swallowed before his master had re-wrapped the other half. That he put away in a metal meat safe, the door of which was pierced with holes. "Half now, half for breakfast," he explained.

As soon as Nero had swallowed every scale and fin of his portion, and licked the plate shining clean, he returned to rub against his master's legs, mewing and purring as loudly as before, but Mr. Murney laughed and said, "No, no, you old tyrant. Enough is as good as a feast! Wash yourself and digest what you ate, and let's have no more nonsense."

Meanwhile Dominic had laid the bundle of kindling in a basket by the fireplace, and, seeing that the hearth held nothing but ashes, had built a fire, using some torn newspaper that lay handy.

"Shall I light the fire for you, sir?" he asked.

"Thank you, my boy! And if you will complete your kindness by fetching me up a bucket of coal, then Nero and I shall do very well indeed."

So Dominic carried the empty coal bucket downstairs

to a bin which stood in the small yard beyond the back door, filled it, and returned. By the time he came back the fire was burning well, and a cheerful warmth filled the book-lined cell, contrasting pleasantly with the crisp cold of the spring evening outside. Nero was now stretched comfortably on the worn hearthrug, his huge black bulk occupying almost the whole of it.

"There, sir," said Dominic. "And now I will leave you, for my mother will be wondering what I am up to."

"Just a moment, my boy," said Mr. Murney. "*I* am wondering too—whether I can interest you in doing a regular job for me?"

"I have a regular job already, sir," said Dominic doubtfully. "At Bentalls, the printers."

"This would be no bar to that," rejoined the bookseller. And he went on to make his proposal, which was that Dominic should call at the bookshop each evening to read aloud the newspaper to Mr. Murney for an hour or so.

Dominic hesitated at first—he really had plenty of uses for his spare time after work, with the spring coming— but he had taken a liking to Mr. Murney and felt sorry for him too—also the bookseller offered most generous pay—so, in the end, the bargain was made.

"You spend more time in that dusty old warren than you do at home!" Mrs. Toole, Dominic's mother, soon began to say fretfully. She was the pensioned widow of a sea-faring man, and time hung heavy on her hands. It was true that Dominic very rapidly came to prefer the cozy maze of the bookshop to his highly polished home and his mother's fretful company. By degrees he took over most of Mr. Murney's outdoor errands, buying food, firing, household needs—which were few—the daily newspaper, and fish for Nero, who soon came to greet him almost as fervently and energetically as he had the bookseller on that first night. Indeed Nero was such a pacer and lacer, such a pusher and thruster, such a twiner and twister about one's feet and legs, and his fat solid bulk was so heavy as he leaned it wishfully against one's shins, that Dominic often marveled that he had never yet tripped his blind master and broken Mr. Murney's neck.

"Patience, patience, keep still, wait just a minute, Nero!" Dominic would cry, hastily unwrapping the herring from its newspaper, while Nero let out raucous howls of hunger, standing on his hind feet, paws on the table, his huge green eyes glaring rapaciously as the delicious fish came in sight. Then, when Nero had been fed, and Mr. Murney sipped what he called his "evening tipple," which was a glass of warm milk with a little brandy in it, they would all arrange themselves for the reading session. Dominic sat on a pile of books, and Mr. Murney in his comfortable lopsided swivel armchair. Nero invariably lay stretched out, busily washing on the hearthrug. First he swept with his tongue down one swelling side, then down the other. Then he attended to the black velvety waistcoat triangle below his chin. Then he did his ears, scrubbing first one, then the other with a front paw. Next he turned to his stomach, both hind feet sticking out like drumsticks while he licked and curried and snuffled at his soft belly fur; then each hind leg was dealt with in turn by elevating it in the air while he stretched his neck and tongue to reach every inch of fur. Last of all came his tail, which he held down with a paw while he combed and smoothed it.

"If we were all as clean as Nero," Mr. Murney sometimes said, smiling, "the world would be a healthier place," and Dominic went pink, thinking of how he, if he were late in the morning, would flick at his face with a damp cloth and forget his ears, bolting for the stairs and breakfast. But Nero, after all, washed when his meal was finished, when there was plenty of time. Sometimes he would suspend his washing for a moment, and, it seemed, listen alertly, while Dominic read some paragraph from the newspaper; he appeared to take every bit as much interest in the day's events as did his master.

Dominic had expected, when he first began the readings, that Mr. Murney would require only the main headlines or news items read to him each evening, but no: he wanted the whole paper, line by line, column by column, even the deaths and births, the law cases, houses for sale, the christening, funerals, and what was said in Parliament. To begin with, Dominic hardly noticed what he read out, but as time went on and one piece of news connected with another, he began to enjoy the reading, and to take almost as much interest in it as the old man did himself.

Every now and then a customer would climb up to the shop while they were in the middle of the paper. Then Mr. Murney would ask Dominic to stop, but to note well what point he had reached, for not a single line of the news must be missed. And when they resumed, he always remembered to a comma exactly where they had got to when they broke off.

At first Dominic had wondered how a blind bookseller could ever find his way about his shop, but he soon came to realize that Mr. Murney knew every volume among his large stock by feel and whereabouts.

"Have you Carlyle's *French Revolution?*" a customer might inquire, and the bookseller would answer at once, "Yes, there are two editions, 1899 and 1910, you will find them on the right of the door, on the second shelf up from the ground, ten volumes from the corner." He knew the age and condition of every book he had in his shop, and the price he was asking for it, and the publisher, and whose name, if any, was written on the flyleaf. Dominic sometimes wondered how he had come by this knowledge, and asked about it, when he had got to know the old man well enough to take the liberty.

"I learned them all before I went blind," Mr. Murney told him. "Now, as you see, I have given up acquiring any more stock."

He did not sell very many books, either, but did not

seem to care about this; indeed, Dominic thought, he often seemed rather sad to have books leave his shop, and would fondle them in a melancholy way before handing them over to a purchaser, as if hoping that they were destined for a kind home and good usage.

During the day, of course, Dominic was at his own work and seldom visited the bookshop; but if he did by any chance run in with a twist of tobacco for Mr. Murney, or some little thing he had thought the old man would like, there would nearly always be a friend or customer there, comfortably talking.

Nero did not take kindly to callers; when friends visited Mr. Murney he would often retreat, sulking, to a nest he had among a mountain of old gramophone records, hidden behind a rampart of books. Or he would depart through the window, for, although he had been born in the shop, and, as Mr. Murney told Dominic, had never set foot in the dangerous street, he had a whole kingdom to visit among the roofs and chimneypots of Robin's Rents. From a lean-to coping below the bookshop window he could leap to a window-ledge, and from that to a fire escape and a blackened plane tree. Often he would be gone for several hours and then, sometimes, Dominic discovered, Mr. Murney did worry about him. For Nero often engaged in fights; he would return from these excursions with a scratched nose and torn ears; sometimes whole patches of fur would be gone. Throwing himself down on the hearth, he would lick and lick at his bleeding scars and scratches until they began to heal, when he would sally out again for more adventures. Yet, Dominic observed, he took care never to be out of doors at the hour of the nightly newspaper reading; then, he was invariably at home, stretched before the fire, or across the table in the rays of the evening sun, indolently purring or grooming himself but, just the same, keeping a careful ear open to all that was said.

Nero never caught mice or rats. There were plenty in the old runways of Rumbury Town, but "He's above that sort of thing," said Mr. Murney. "Wouldn't demean himself. He leaves hunting to other cats."

Nero accepted Dominic far more kindly than he did the other visitors; possibly because Dominic brought his fish. Just once, on a single occasion, there came a coolness between them.

Dominic had begun to notice, as he went to and fro along Robin's Rents between his home, at the canal end, and his place of work, near All Hallows Church, and Mr. Murney's shop halfway along the street, that a famished, apparently homeless kitten was to be seen, here and there about the neighborhood, making do as best it could on scraps of waste near the docks, or on what it could scavenge from trash cans, or on the charity of office girls who sometimes, eating their sandwich lunches in All Hallows churchyard, would fling it a cheese rind or a crust. The kitten was striped, gray, black, and tabby, and would have been quite handsome if it had not been so scrawny, draggled, and saucer-eyed. Buying a herring for fat pampered Nero at the quayside, Dominic would sometimes beg a cod head, or spare a penny for a few sprats, which the kitten received and devoured with famished haste and ferocity. After a few weeks it learned to look out for Dominic and to follow him along the street, dodging through the traffic as if it had twenty lives to spare, not just nine. And finally one day, ever hungry and hopeful, it followed Dominic up the stone steps to Mr. Murney's shop and even, letting out a series of pleading squeaks, through the doorway and into the bookshop. Not to remain there long, though!

Even across several ramparts of books, Nero seemed able to detect an intruder. Like a silent sack of coal he dropped down from his sunny table and trundled through the lanes of books, with his two-inch fur standing up all over his body like the quills of a black and furious porcupine. As he came he let out a dreadful wailing droning snarl which must have made the kitten's bones almost melt in their sockets with fright. It did not wait for any closer acquaintance with Nero, but bolted away down the stairs as if seven devils were after it. Nero paused, glaring a moment, in the doorway, sniffed disdainfully at the floor, gave Dominic a look—such a look!—then, slowly, switching his tail from side to side, he turned and paced back to the hearth.

"What in the world is taking place?" inquired Mr. Murney from his swivel-chair. "What has upset old Nero?"

"A kitten came in. It was only a kitten," nervously

explained Dominic. "The poor little thing lives in the street—I wondered if perhaps—perhaps you and Nero—might have had room here for another cat. It's only a little tiny one—"

"Oh, dear me, no," said Mr. Murney decidedly. "No, Nero would never stand for that. He couldn't consider sharing his place with another cat. No, I'm afraid that would never do."

"No, I can see that," said Dominic sadly.

"Perhaps your mother would adopt the kitten?" suggested the old man.

"She can't abide cats, sir."

So Dominic continued to feed the kitten, when he had a scrap to spare, or a penny to buy it a few sprats; and the kitten continued to follow him trustfully, but it did not come up the stairs again. It would remain down at the street door, looking up after him wistfully as he ascended with his bundle of firewood, and the newspaper, and Nero's fish.

And, for three whole weeks after that episode, Nero would not come near Dominic, but growled at him, and hissed, and spat, and would only receive his dinner from his own master. By degrees, however, he became more friendly, and at last treated Dominic again as if the unfortunate incident had been forgotten.

Nowadays, Mr. Murney hardly ever went out any more. He left his errands entirely to Dominic, who worried a little about the old man.

"Don't you think you ought to take a bit of exercise,

have some fresh air sometimes, sir? You could get one of those guide dogs to lead you about?"

"Guide dogs? Oh, good gracious, no, I could never do that," said Mr. Murney. "Where would I keep it?" Nero let out a low growl at the very idea. "We don't care for dogs," Mr. Murney said. "A dog would knock over my books."

The old man seemed perfectly content to stay in his shop. "I get plenty of fresh air opening the window for Nero to go in and out," he said. "And I see my customers and friends; they give me sufficient news from the world outside, as well as what you read me, my dear Dominic."

Both Nero and his owner seemed to set more and more store by Dominic's daily reading of the paper. Every word was taken in, it seemed, and inwardly digested. Even during Nero's three-weeks' displeasure he never missed a reading, but paid close attention, with his front paws tightly tucked and curled under his chest, and his eyes narrowed to slits.

Now and then Dominic couldn't help wondering if perhaps Mr. Murney had some hidden reason for wishing to hear the news. Could he be a retired bank robber, who had, hidden among his books, all the proceeds from some tremendous smash-and-grab raid, and was now waiting for the rest of the gang to come out of jail? That would account for his never leaving the shop. Perhaps the other members of the gang did not know where he had hidden himself.

Or could he be a spy? Or a political refugee from some

foreign land, escaping the vengeance of their secret police for assassinating a dictator? Dominic did not entirely believe in any of these theories, but, just the same, when some strange men with a truck came along the street one Sunday, selling firewood, and asked if Dominic knew who lived on the first floor above the die-stamp shop, Dominic told them that it was a young lady who gave piano lessons. He said that his mother would like a load of wood (which was not true, for she detested open fires and had only an electric heater); he paid for the wood himself, and laboriously shifted it, barrow by barrowful, to the old man's back yard.

Afterward Dominic wondered why he had told such a lie to the wood vendors. But he had grown very fond of the old man, and did not wish him to be upset by any outside disturbances. They lived peacefully together, the old man and Nero; nothing ought to interfere with their tranquillity.

Something did, though.

One autumn evening—October thirty-first, it was—the wind was dashing scattered plane leaves from All Hallows churchyard about the street, when Dominic, rather later than his usual habit, came hurrying along Robin's Rents to the door by the die-stamp shop. Traffic had died away and dusk was falling. As usual the kitten waited for him hopefully by the foot of the stairs, and he dropped it a cheese rind, saying, "Sorry, mate, that's all I have today. I'll try to get some sprats for you tomorrow."

The kitten did not complain. Thankfully it fell on the scrap of cheese rind, and Dominic went whistling up the stairs.

Nero was waiting to greet him, as usual, just inside the door, his great green eyes lambent as traffic lights, and he twined heavily about Dominic's legs all the way to the table and his dish.

"Watch out! You nearly had me over then!" warned Dominic, wondering how much Nero weighed; over thirty pounds, he would be ready to bet.

Nero fed, Dominic made up the fire with a hunk of wood and a shovelful of coal. Soon they were all settled down, the three of them, Dominic squatting on his pile of books, Mr. Murney relaxed in his swivel chair, Nero carefully cleaning the last silvery smears of herring off his whiskers.

According to custom, Dominic worked steadily through the paper, from the left-hand front page headline about a trade conference in Geneva, on, across the front page with news of armed hostilities in Central America, hurricanes in the Caribbean, marriage of a Spanish princess, and a typhoid outbreak in Scotland. Now and then he was obliged to turn to the back page in order to finish off front page stories that were continued there; then he went to page two, for more foreign news; then page three, home news. Further home news on pages four and five; then the arts page, with articles about plays and paintings and opera, then on to the center pages which contained ed-

UP THE CHIMNEY DOWN

itorial opinions and letters and articles on world affairs.

Dominic was a little tempted to skip a line here or there; today was his birthday, and he had a few friends coming in later, despite his mother's grumbles; he wanted to be sure he arrived home in time to let them in. But he had never skipped while reading to Mr. Murney, and he did not really intend to now; the notion simply brushed his mind and was dismissed.

On he read, through the financial and city pages (the only part he found really boring, for so much of the contents consisted of figures). But Mr. Murney always paid careful attention, even here. He had explained to Dominic that his income did not come only from the bookshop; he had made some investments as well. "Not much, but enough. They go up and down, and I like to follow what happens to them," he said.

At last they were through the city pages, and on to the back page, which, of course, had been partly culled already. But there were small paragraphs here and there which had not been read; Dominic carefully singled these out. The very last of all, at the foot of the right-hand column, was a small story headed:

STRANGE OCCURRENCE IN THE COTSWOLDS.

" 'A Cotswold farmer, James Mugg,' " Dominic read aloud, " 'whose car had broken down, was taking a midnight shortcut home through the ruins of Gletbury Abbey, on the side of Swode Hill, when he heard the sound of mournful chanting, and was astonished to see a procession of cats carrying a bier. Hardly able to believe his eyes he followed the cortège, and was in time to see the cats lower the coffin into a previously dug grave. Before the coffin was covered with earth he observed a gold crown embroidered on the black velvet pall draped over it.

" 'Returning the next day to what he thought was the same spot, Mr. Mugg was unable to discover any trace of the grave—' "

Suddenly Dominic became aware of the charged and prickling silence that seemed to surround his voice. Both listeners were sitting bolt upright, Nero on the hearthrug, Mr. Murney in his swivel chair.

"I beg your pardon, my dear Dominic," said Mr. Murney, "but would you mind reading that again?"

" 'A Cotswold farmer, James Mugg . . .' " read Dominic. Through the newspaper, as he held it, he could almost feel Nero's whiskers vibrating, and see the blaze of his emerald eyes.

" '. . . The next day . . . Mr. Mugg was unable to discover any trace of the grave . . .' "

"A crown?" interrupted Mr. Murney. "It quite definitely says a *crown* on the pall?"

"A gold crown on the black velvet pall."

Suddenly there came a blinding flash of lightning and a rolling clap of thunder.

"THEN," cried Nero in a loud and terrible voice, "old Tybalt's dead, and *I'm the King of the cats!*" and with one bound he was away up the chimney, leaving behind him a huge cloud of black billowing soot, and a strong smell of sulphur.

For several minutes after that Mr. Murney and Dominic remained in silence, facing one another over the ash-strewn hearthrug. Presently Dominic began, rather mechanically, to trample out a few glowing sparks on the rug; then he fetched the hearth brush and coal shovel and swept the area clean. Still neither of them spoke a word. With a deep sigh, Mr. Murney lay back in his chair and rested his head on one hand. He looked, Dominic thought, very old and tired and solitary.

Wondering whether to say anything, Dominic waited a little longer. Did the old man know about Nero? Surely he must have known.

At last, nervously clearing his throat, Dominic said, "Would—would you wish me to come in tomorrow, sir? And—and read the paper?"

Rousing himself, the bookseller answered sadly, "If you have time, Dominic. If you have time. One must not expect the young to wait on the old forever."

And then he muttered, mostly to himself, something that Dominic did not catch, in which "bookshop" and "legacy" were the only audible words.

"I—I really like coming here, Mr. Murney," said Dominic. "I've learned such a lot—" but the old man did not seem to be attending, and so, a little troubled, but also mindful of his friends and his party, Dominic edged his way through the barricades of books toward the entrance, resolving to come early tomorrow, and spend a good couple of hours with Mr. Murney.

He opened the door.

And the striped scrawny kitten, which had been sitting outside, dashed straight through the opening and among the piles of books, as if it had a right to be there.

Up the Chimney
Down

This is the story of Clove and Cinnamon, the two clever sisters who outwitted Mrs. McMurk, the witch—and of their grandmother, old Mrs. Baker, who made cakes for the winds.

Listen, then.

In the middle of the town of New York there is a building thirty stories high. Gray as a boulder, sharp as a dragon's tooth, it stands by the park, pointing at the sky. And, in the middle of it, there is a secret room that everybody has forgotten, a room that was made without doors or windows, by mistake, ever so long ago.

In this room lives the witch, Mrs. McMurk, among her scrambled belongings. The people who live below her don't know she is there; nor do the people above. Nor do the ones on either side. How does she get in and out? Up the chimney, of course. How did she find the room in the first place? Who knows. Perhaps one day she floated down the chimney like a withered leaf. Per-

118

haps a rat told her about it. Witches know all kinds of things.

Anyway, there she is, high up above the noise of the city traffic. Every day, all day, down below, it goes to and fro, to and fro. And every day Mrs. McMurk, before this story began, used to go out hunting for new treasure. The people in the streets often used to see her—an old lady dressed from top to toe in newspaper. She had newspaper wrapped around her legs and tied with string, a newspaper hat, newspaper cloak, newspaper skirt. Always, rain or shine, she carried her umbrella. She could be seen poking around garbage cans, peering into boxes left on the pavement, squinting under parked cars or trucks; or, in the most expensive shops. Every now and then she would grab some object, with a quick, spiderish snatch, and stuff it into her umbrella. You'd think the umbrella would have been stuffed and bulging; but no, it was always empty. When she dropped things in, they vanished.

Very often Mrs. McMurk would visit a supermarket. These, and big department stores, she loved best of all. She could happily spend hours and hours wandering up and down the aisles, listening to the dreamy music they play there, and putting tins, packets, cartons, boxes, bottles, fruits, vegetables, jewels, dresses, hairbrushes, bath essence, and bottles of scent into her shopping cart.

Did the witch pay for these articles? By no means! When she arrived at the cash register, she would lay out all her things on the counter, then put into her mouth a long green cigarette (ignoring NO SMOKING signs) and focus her violently squinting red eyes on the cigarette tip, which at once glowed red. Mrs. McMurk then blew a cloud of green smoke at the cashier, who thereupon fell into a dreamy doze, while the witch packed all her acquisitions neatly into a shopping bag and strolled out of the shop without paying. Outside, the shopping bag went into her umbrella, and before the cashier had woken up, Mrs. McMurk would be miles away, flying through the air, holding on to the handle of her umbrella.

The witch always kept a servant—somebody to tidy up her roomful of cluttered treasures, to answer the telephone, make the bed, cook the dinner, and wash the dishes (for witches hate running water). Her usual habit was to catch the servants young, train them to obey her orders and fall in with her ways, then, later on, when they grew large enough to be disobedient, she would eat them and replace them.

One rainy day when Mrs. McMurk had just eaten her latest servant (a fat, rebellious boy called Bosseye), she went out looking for a replacement.

First she glided into a supermarket and collected a number of delights—a frozen cake, and a hundred oranges, and a magnetic pot holder, and a new broom, and a flowering chrysanthemum, and a whole Dutch cheese, and a head of celery, and a chiming clock, and a paintbox, and twenty pairs of tights, and some clothespins.

Then she went to the checkout counter, ready to play her usual trick with the green cigarette. Ahead of her was a nice little dumpy motherly old person with white hair and a double folding stroller under one arm. The old person was plainly going to do a whole lot of baking, for her shopping cart was loaded right up to the brim with flour and butter and eggs and yeast and milk and all the spices you can think of—mace, cinnamon, nutmeg, cloves, allspice, ginger, caraway (and many others I haven't time to mention) besides brown sugar, white sugar, and honey.

"Looks like you're going to be busy, Mrs. Baker," said the checkout girl.

"I'm always busy," replied Mrs. Baker. Which was true, for she had a little bread and cake shop in Bagel Street, not far from the supermarket, just around the corner and along the block. Above the window swung a gold sign: V. Baker & Daughter, Bakers to the Winds. Mrs. Vanilla Baker and her daughter, Nutmeg, were the Official Bread and Cake Suppliers to all the winds of the world; and, as there are hundreds of winds all the way around the compass from north-north-north-west to north-north-north-east, the mother and daughter had their hands full. Every day at tea time they went into the street with their trays of macaroons, sponge fingers, sticky buns, éclairs, and Maids of Honor. All these things they tossed up in the air, and the wind snatched them and carried them away like feathers; for the wind loves sweet things. And so long as Mrs. Baker and her daughter went on feeding the wind, there were very few severe storms or gales, for these only occur when the wind grows hungry. If—as sometimes happened—the wind was not very hungry and did not take all the cakes on the trays, Mrs. Baker would sell what remained to ordinary customers, and there were always plenty of these waiting in a long line outside the door, for Mrs. Baker's cakes were famous all over the city, and, indeed, all over the world.

The witch in the supermarket stared hard at Mrs. Baker's shopping cart. But what interested her was not the load of flour, eggs, and spices, but the two baby girls who were perched, gazing eagerly about themsleves, in the upper basket of the cart.

"Brought your granddaughters today, I see, Mrs. Baker," said the checkout girl, neatly packing flour and eggs and butter into a huge carrier bag.

"Dear little Cinnamon and Clove, yes," said Mrs. Baker. "An airing's good for them, and my daughter Nutmeg can get on with raising the first batch of dough. Anyway they can't start learning the business too early, for they'll be taking it on, by and by."

"How old are they now?" asked the checkout girl, slipping in a last vanilla bean.

"Six months, bless them," said Mrs. Baker, taking out her purse to pay. Then she unfolded the folding stroller and popped the twins into it, side by side, before picking up her heavy bag of groceries.

But while she turned to do this, quick as a flash, the witch leaned forward, whisked little Clove out of the stroller, and replaced her with a head of celery.

Nobody saw this happen, for the checkout girl was telling Mrs. Baker how much she liked chocolate éclairs, and Mrs. Baker was explaining how busy she and her daughter would be all day because of a whole College of Winds who would be visiting the city with their Deacon, and every one of them would need feeding.

The only person to notice the witch snatch little Clove was her twin sister, Cinnamon—who was so startled and horrified at the deed that she just gazed, with open mouth and round blue eyes full of fright, as she saw her sister stuffed into the witch's umbrella and replaced in the stroller by a head of celery.

Mrs. Baker, having noticed nothing, said, "Well, goodbye, Hilda, see you tomorrow," picked up her heavy bag, and steered the stroller out of the supermarket. By this time the head of celery had changed into a likeness of little Clove, so that no one, except her own sister, could see the difference.

Meanwhile the witch was so delighted with her own cleverness that she absentmindedly paid in real money for all the things she had collected. (She always carried plenty of money because, while wandering about the city, she had the habit of waving her umbrella over pools and fountains, into which, for some reason, people often drop silver coins; when she did this, all the coins would fly to her umbrella like pins to a magnet; so she could perfectly well have paid for her groceries all the time. Just the same, she was very annoyed when she realized what she had done.)

Mrs. Baker plodded home to the baker's shop with her heavy load, and put the twins into their playpen. But while little Cinnamon began at once to crawl about and play with her toys, the imitation twin who was just a head of celery sat still as a dummy in her corner, and neither spoke nor moved.

"I can't think what ails that child!" exclaimed her mother several times during the day. Her sister, who knew very well what was the matter, cried and grieved, hour after hour, but, since she could not yet talk, she could not explain what had happened. And, even if she had, who would have believed her?

In ten minutes the witch's umbrella had borne her up onto the roof of the tall gray spiky building in which her room lay hidden. She landed by the chimney stack, snapped her umbrella shut, sucked in her breath, cried "Down the chimney, down!" and immediately slipped down her own chimney, like a snake into a crack in the rock.

There she was, safe at home.

And all the time the traffic down below went to and fro, to and fro.

Little Clove, who had been quite dazed by the suddenness of what had happened, found herself dumped in the witch's parlor, amongst a clutter of stolen treasures— dragons' teeth, X-ray machines, seven-league boots, digital watches, diamond tiaras, pictures by famous painters worth thousands of pounds, velvet dresses, and bulletproof waistcoats. The room was terribly untidy.

"Now," said the witch, poking little Clove with her umbrella. "You are my servant, and your name is Celery." Mrs. McMurk spoke in witch language, which sounds like the leafy branches of trees hissing in a high wind. "The first thing you can do," she went on, "is to tidy up this mess. Then sweep the dust. Then you can wash my dirty laundry—there's the heap of clothes and that's the washing machine in the corner. Then you can cook the dinner. There's some stuff in the refrigerator. If you disobey me, or don't work hard enough, I shall beat you with my umbrella. So, behave yourself! If you don't, I shall eat you, as I did my last servant. Those are his bones in the other corner. You can put them down the rubbish disposal chute. Now I'm going to sleep, don't disturb me." And Mrs. McMurk lay down on a pile of mink and ermine cloaks. Soon she was fast asleep and snoring.

And all the time the traffic down below went to and fro, to and fro.

Little Clove, now called Celery, sat looking about her in despair. She was only six months old. How could she tidy up all that mess? Two huge tears slowly filled her eyes and then rolled down her cheeks.

After a while the witch woke up.

"Why didn't you do as I told you?" she hissed angrily, seeing that her treasures hadn't been tidied, and the dinner was not cooked, and the dirty laundry still lay in its heap, and so did the bones of Bosseye.

Poor little Celery got beaten with the umbrella. Not for the last time.

And all the while the traffic down below went to and fro.

Far away, Celery's sister, Cinnamon, felt the blows, and she cried bitterly.

And the substitute baby, who was really a head of celery, tumbled onto its side and lay without moving. Nutmeg, the mother, let out a shriek.

"Oh! My baby! My baby is sick, call the doctor!" And then she wailed, "My baby has died!" Many were the tears, deep was the sorrow in the baker's shop. Little Cinnamon wept too, but at least she knew that her sister was not dead.

In her room far away Mrs. McMurk was beating Celery yet again.

"How can you expect the child to work for you when you haven't taught her how?" angrily stuttered a computer that stood between a grandfather clock and a sack of oranges. In its indignation it threw out yards of paper.

What it said was true, as the witch knew. So, irritably and with many slaps and thumps, she taught poor little Celery how to load the washing machine, and how to sweep and dust, and tidy up the jumbled roomful of treasures, and how to cook the frozen food which was what Mrs. McMurk mostly ate.

"I'm hungry too!" wept Celery.

"You? Why should you have anything to eat?"

"If you don't give the child food she will die," pointed out the computer, coughing out another twenty feet of paper.

"Oh, very well, you can eat oranges," grumbled the

witch. So little Celery sucked half a dozen oranges and then cried herself to sleep. Far away, Cinnamon, in her wooden cradle, had a strange dream of a room filled with machines, and shining jewels, and piles of other things for which she did not know the names.

"Oh, where are you?" called Cinnamon inside her heart, for she could not talk yet.

And, coming from far away, she heard inside her heart the answer, "I love you, I love you, I am here!"

"Where is *here*?"

"I don't know . . ."

"Come back, come back!"

"I can't come back. I don't know how!"

Since they could not talk in words yet, the sisters could exchange only very simple messages. *I love you, come back! I love you, I can't come back!* Still, these messages were much better than nothing, and comforted them a little, as the days and the weeks went by.

Slowly, the sisters grew. Each of them learned well what she was taught. Celery learned to look after the witch's belongings, wind the grandfather clock, sort the jewels, answer the telephone, brew wolfsbane wine; while Cinnamon watched her mother and grandmother bake bread and cakes for the winds. Slowly, at the steady speed of human children, Cinnamon picked up words and sentences and how to talk. All the words that she learned she passed on to her sister in dreams and messages from heart to heart. So, as well as witches' language, Celery also learned human talk, and, by slow stages, she became able to describe to her sister the strange place that she was in.

"Every day my mistress goes out shopping and leaves me alone. I'm alone now."

"What is she like, your mistress?"

"She has red eyes that squint across her nose. And gray-green hair, long and straight. She is all dressed in newspaper. And she is very, very fat, huge, like a pumpkin only much, much bigger. But before she goes out she rubs ointment down her sides. Then she grows thin, thinner than a pencil. She takes her umbrella and orders it: 'Up the chimney down!' Then the umbrella flies up the chimney, quick as a bird, with my mistress holding on to the handle."

"Well," said Cinnamon, "why can't you escape while she is out?"

"There are no doors or windows to this room."

"Where is the room?"

"How can I tell? I can often hear helicopters flying overhead. And all the time I can hear the traffic down below, going to and fro, to and fro."

"Could you climb up the chimney?"

"It is much too narrow."

"Well then," said Cinnamon, after thinking for a while, "you must steal the ointment, and rub it on yourself. Perhaps a broom would do instead of the umbrella."

This seemed a very clever idea to Celery. But she realized that it would not be easy to carry out. The witch always kept her little pot of ointment in a bag tied to her belt. And when she slept she locked up the bag in a steel cupboard, and tucked the key to the cupboard under her tongue; it never slipped out, however loudly she snored.

"Well, could you find out how she makes the ointment, and make some for yourself?" suggested Cinnamon, when her sister told her of this difficulty one day while the witch was out, and the two sisters were talking, heart to heart.

"She never lets me see her make it. When she is at work on a new potful she lights one of her green cigarettes and puffs the smoke at me. Then I can't keep awake, I fall asleep, and by the time I wake she has made the paste and put it in the pot. But," said Celery, "I think the paste must be made from leeks and garlic and fennel and hemlock and moss and green ginger and gum and rum. Those are the things she brings back before she makes a new batch of paste, and they are always gone by the time I wake."

"Humph," said Cinnamon. "Just repeat that list again, will you?"

"Leeks and fennel and garlic and hemlock and moss and green ginger and gum and rum."

Then the witch dropped down the chimney with a new load of stolen treasures, and the two sisters had to stop talking.

Little Cinnamon was now considered old enough to make simple things in the bakery: pancakes and flapjacks and icing for small cakes; and she was sometimes sent out around the corner to the supermarket on her own, when her mother and grandmother were hard at work and unexpectedly ran out of saffron or cochineal.

Cinnamon had a little money of her own, which the wind had dropped into her hand while she swept the pavement. So next time she was sent out, she bought leeks and garlic and fennel and green ginger and gum and rum; she picked up some moss and some hemlock leaves in the park, and when she had a little time to herself at home, she boiled all these things together and made them into a paste. It was green and thick and smelled very strong.

Just when it was done, her grandmother called, "Cinnamon! Cinnamon! Come here a moment, dear, and help me pull on the strudel pastry."

Cinnamon ran to help her grandmother. Strudel pastry has to be pulled and stretched out by two people, until it is as thin as muslin; then it is rolled up to keep cool. Cinnamon and her granny pulled the pastry in the little yard behind the kitchen, where there was more room.

When Cinnamon went back into the kitchen, she was greatly dismayed to find that her little bowl of green paste was nowhere to be seen. And her mother wore a very perplexed expression.

"What in the world did you put into that green icing, child? I spread it over a batch of queen cakes, and they all rose up and flew out of the window!"

Cinnamon wondered whether to tell her mother and grandmother about the search for her lost sister. But, she thought, suppose I never find her? They think poor Clove is dead; they have almost forgotten her. It will only upset them all over again. It will be better if I don't tell them.

"It must have been that batch of green ginger," her mother said. "I believe it was beginning to ferment. Don't use any more of it."

"No, I won't," said Cinnamon sadly.

This was an easy promise to keep, for she had used up all the things she had bought. And she had used up all her money too.

Meanwhile Celery, in the witch's parlor, unhappy and lonely, had learned how to talk to the computer. When she was alone she tapped on its buttons, and out would come a ribbon of paper with an answer to her questions.

"Should I ever escape from the witch's parlor?" she would ask, and the computer would reply "yes or no," for it always saw both sides of a question.

"What will happen if I don't escape?"

"The witch will eat you as she ate the others," replied the computer.

"What others?"

"The ones that she ate."

"When will she do that?"

"When you weigh seventy-seven pounds."

Among the other objects in the witch's parlor there were some bathroom scales. In a fright, Celery ran to it and weighed herself. But, thank goodness, she didn't weigh anything like seventy-seven pounds yet. All she got to eat was oranges, and they, though full of vitamins, are not fattening. And she did not get fed every day, only when Mrs. McMurk remembered to bring some oranges back with her.

But still, the knowledge that, if she stayed, she was bound to get eaten sooner or later, made Celery more anxious to escape than ever.

"How does the witch mix her ointment?" she asked the computer one day.

"Either by hand or in the blender," it answered.

Unfortunately at that moment the witch shot down the chimney with a four-poster French bed, and a fountain and a flying fish. When she noticed that Celery had been asking the computer questions, the witch beat the child vigorously with her umbrella, and what was worse, she picked up a meat mallet and smashed the computer into forty pieces.

"Now!" she said, "you scheming little wretch, you can drop all those pieces down the garbage chute. Then clean the silver. Polish the brass. Rub up the gold. Make the bed and cook my frozen pizza. And don't let me catch you talking to the flying fish."

And all the time the traffic down below went to and fro, to and fro.

Poor Celery rubbed her bruises with a bit of orange peel. She made up the four-poster bed with satin sheets and velvet blankets. She put the flying fish into the fountain, where it swam around very slowly and sadly. She polished the silver and cooked frozen pizza for the witch's supper and ate oranges for her own. Mrs. McMurk took a short nap in the four-poster. Then she rubbed herself with green ointment until she was thin as a stick of spaghetti. Grabbing the umbrella she commanded it: "Up the chimney down!" Immediately the closed umbrella whisked away up the chimney, hauling the witch after it.

Half an hour after she left, the telephone rang. Celery picked up the receiver, which was carved out of a large pink pearl.

"Mrs. McMurk's residence," Celery said in witch language, as she had been trained.

"Hello, this is the Senior Sorceror of Sicily," said the voice at the other end. "Can that be old Misery McMurk? I saw your name in the *Devil's Directory*."

Celery was about to reply, "She's not in," when the flying fish leapt clean out of the fountain, did a loop in the air, and returned to the water. This, for some reason, changed her mind, and she replied, "Yes it is!"

"Well, fancy that, old Misery, haven't seen you since college days! I'll be flying over your roof in a couple of hours, can I drop in for a cup of wolfsbane?"

"Do, that would be very pleasant!" said Celery. "And, as you are coming, could you be kind enough to bring me some leeks, garlic, fennel, hemlock, moss, green ginger, gum, and rum? I've been plagued lately by rheumatism and haven't been able to get out much."

"No trouble at all," said the Senior Sorcerer, and he rang off. What'll I ever do, thought Celery, if he arrives before Mrs. McMurk gets back?

Luckily the witch arrived first, with some Crown Derby and a lot of video games. She was delighted to hear that a visitor was expected, for she had very few friends.

"Tidy away all those emerald necklaces and heat up some frozen coffee cake," she said. "Be ready to take the Senior Sorceror's hat and galoshes when he comes."

Celery took not only his hat and galoshes but also the small leather sack he carried.

"I brought along the things you wanted, old Misery," he hissed genially. "Sorry to hear you've been plagued with aches and pains. What I always recommend is—"

"Aches and pains?" Mrs. McMurk was puzzled. "Who says I've got aches and pains—?"

Luckily at that moment the flying fish leapt clean out of its water and landed, flapping, on a Stradivarius violin. The Senior Sorceror (who had long white moustaches and looked himself rather like a fountain turned to ice) politely helped catch the fish and put it back in the water again. "Awkward things!" he said. "Too bony, and too much trouble, in my opinion."

"Delicious flavor though," said Mrs. McMurk.

Celery stared at the beautiful pink and silver flying fish in horror. Was Mrs. McMurk going to eat it? Would she, Celery, have to cook it? What a dreadful thought.

"Fetch the wolfsbane wine, girl," said the witch, "and then make yourself scarce behind the grand piano, and don't eavesdrop."

Celery brought the big flask of ruby wine and two little gold-encrusted glasses. Then she crouched behind the grand piano. She had every intention of listening, but unfortunately the two old friends began puffing on long green cigars, the smoke drifted all over the room, and in no time Celery had fallen fast asleep.

When she woke up it was because the drinkers, grown rather merry, were singing:

"There is a cavern in the town, in the town,
 Where the witch doctors sit them down,
  sit them down,
 Where mandrake brandy sparkles clear
 And toasts are drunk in nightshade beer—"

They reeled about the room, waving their glasses, and the Senior Sorceror, seizing Mrs. McMurk's umbrella, shouted, "Down the chimney up!" Instantly the umbrella shot open and began dragging him toward the fireplace.

"Don't do that, you idiot!" creaked the witch, hiccuping as she snatched the umbrella from him and thumped it shut. "It's *up* the chimney *down*, not down the chimney up! You'd not have a shred of skin left, let alone not having smeared yourself with hemlock paste. What the devil, now, did I do with that pot of ointment?"

Celery waited in dread for the Senior Sorceror to say something about the bag of ingredients he had kindly brought, but he was too full of wolfsbane wine, and was busily hunting for his galoshes, which he had already put on, back to front and on the wrong feet. They were magic ones, which he used in the same way as Mrs. McMurk used her umbrella. She, discovering the pot of ointment

135

inside her newspaper hat, liberally anointed herself and her friend, then said, "I'll walk you to the bus stop," grabbing hold of his wrist with one skinny claw and her umbrella with the other.

"Wash the glasses, you little toad!" she called over her shoulder to Celery, and ordered the umbrella, "Up the chimney down, and be quick about it."

Next minute, both revellers had vanished up the chimney, and Celery, filled with excitement and joy, was calling to her sister,

"Tell me quick, how did you mix up the hemlock and the other things?"

"I boiled the leeks with the garlic and fennel and hemlock . . . then I put in the moss and green ginger. Then I pounded it all with a pestle."

Celery peeled and chopped and boiled and mixed with a beating heart, as if her life depended on her speed— which it very likely did, for if the witch came home and found out, she would probably have been squashed like a cockroach.

That very same day, Mrs. Baker said to her granddaughter: "There's a Convocation of Trade Winds coming to the town today, dearie. Sweep the street from end to end, love, so that when the winds come to pick up their cakes, they don't also pick up a whole nasty mess of chocolate wrappers and voting papers and ice-cream containers and apple cores."

So little Cinnamon put on her pink pinafore and went

out with a broom, as she had often done before, to sweep the street from end to end.

"What a good tidy little girl," said the winds flying over, waiting hungrily and impatiently for it to be tea time. "Look at her there, sweeping and cleaning the street, and packing all the rubbish so neatly into the trash basket. She ought to have a reward for that. Don't you think so?" the winds asked each other. "What should it be?"

And as they flew over they called down to Cinnamon:

"Child, child, sweeping the street,
Making the pavement clean and neat
What is your wish, what is your will?
All your requirements we'll gladly fulfil!"

Cinnamon heard the winds' cry, but she was not paying much attention, for she was in such a state of excitement and worry, wondering, as she swept, whether Clove would be able to mix up the magic ingredients in the right way, wondering whether the witch would catch her at it, wondering whether Clove would need the witch's umbrella to go up the chimney, whether it would bring her here, to Bagel Street, how it would know the way, whether the witch would follow, and so many more questions of the same kind that her head was buzzing like an overloaded refrigerator. So she put no heed to the winds and their kind offer as they flew to and fro.

Cinnamon worked her way along the short street,

sweeping the rubbish into piles, then taking them, load by load, and squashing them into the large trash basket at the corner. But what was her annoyance, when she came back with her fourth load, to see that an old woman was rummaging in the basket and tossing half its contents back onto the pavement! She seemed to be searching for something right down at the bottom, poking with her umbrella.

"Don't do that!" Cinnamon started to shout indignantly, from halfway along the street—when something about the old lady's appearance began to nibble at her attention.

The old lady was dressed all in newspaper. Newspaper wrapped around her legs, tied with string, newspaper hat, newspaper skirt, newspaper cloak. She was amazingly thin—thin as a length of hosepipe. She had green hair, straight and limp as the leaves of leeks. Her eyes were fiery red, brighter than hot coals. They met and crossed over her nose in a wild squint. She had a hooky nose and carried an umbrella.

Surely it must be the witch, thought Cinnamon. It must be Mrs. McMurk. There couldn't be two old ladies with green hair and red eyes. But no, Clove always tells me that Mrs. McMurk is very fat. No, it can't be she.

Cinnamon studied the old lady. She was hooking all kinds of things out of the wastebasket with her umbrella, inspecting them, then flinging them untidily about the street. And she was singing in a loud, raucous voice:

"There is a cavern in the town, in the town
Where spooks and spectres sit them down,
   sit them down,
There witches sip at hemlock tea
And toadstool crisps are passed out free!"

Every now and then the old lady did a little hop, skip
and jump. She seemed to be in a very cheerful frame of
mind.

It must be my sister's witch, thought Cinnamon. And
then she remembered that the magic ointment, rubbed
on to whisk her up the chimney, made Mrs. McMurk
thin as a celery stalk. It *is* the witch! Oh, if only I can
somehow get that magic ointment away from her!

So, instead of running like a hare, as most people
would at sight of the fearsome old lady, Cinnamon tiptoed
closer and closer, unnoticed by the witch who was busy
rummaging in the trash basket.

"*Somewhere* in here," she was mumbling to herself,
"somewhere in here I can smell a gold watch that some
fool has accidentally thrown away. I can hear it tick!
Search it out, my dear umbrella—sniff, smell, scent it
out, hook it up, fetch it for your mistress. Snuff it out
for old Misery McMurk!"

It *is* the witch, thought Cinnamon joyfully, and she
edged closer and closer. The winds flew past again, singing:

"Child, child, sweeping the street,
   Making the tarmac clean and neat

Tell us your wish! Come, decide!
All your needs we'll be glad to provide!"

But Cinnamon paid no attention to them, she was so absorbed in watching the witch.

Suddenly a gold watch flew up out of a nest of dirty tissues, and clung like a bee to the witch's umbrella.

"Aha! Aha!" she cackled. "Fine umbrella! Clever umbrella! For that, you shall have new silver ribs and a new cover of Chinese Tribute silk!" And, after gloating and chuckling over the watch, which was an old and handsome one, she dropped it inside the umbrella. Then she looked up, and what met her eyes? Little Cinnamon, just the other side of the trash basket.

The witch let out a terrible hiss, like steam escaping from a boiler.

"Sssssssssssss! Ssssssslave! Dissssobedient sssssslave! What are you doing here? Why aren't you at home cleaning the silver? What are you doing out here in the street?"

For of course she had long ago forgotten the fact that her servant had a twin sister. She thought that Cinnamon was Celery. Full of rage, she leaned across the trash basket and hooked the strap of Cinnamon's pinafore with the crook of her umbrella.

But one of the winds, flitting by, wailed: "Hey, brothers! Look what that ugly old hag is doing to our dear little girl who sweeps the street, whose mother and grandmother give us cake for tea! Blow her! Blast her! Puff her! Waft her!"

And he himself blew such a violent blast against the trash basket that it bounced up in the air and turned upside down on top of the witch.

"Help! Let me out of here!" yelled Mrs. McMurk, struggling furiously inside the wire mesh basket, which was very heavy. She pushed it over and rolled along the pavement, still inside the basket, kicking and cursing. Her language was dreadful. But luckily it was all in witch talk, and sounded like a whistling kettle.

Cinnamon started away when the witch hooked her pinafore strap. The strap tore loose. But Cinnamon did not run away, though she was very frightened indeed. If Clove can endure this awful old woman, she thought, I can. She ran along beside Mrs. McMurk, as the trash basket rolled along the street, strewing out its untidy contents. Broken combs flew out—empty Coke cans—beer bottles—squashed bananas—dead batteries—crumpled newspapers—sticky paper bags—even nastier things— then, suddenly, a little white marble pot, about the size of an orange. Its top fell off. Inside the pot, Cinnamon could see a small amount of green paste.

Just imagine how quickly she snatched up that little pot!

Without hesitating a moment, she scooped out a fingerful of the green ointment and rubbed it all the way up her right side, from ankle to ear. Then another fingerful down the left side, from ear to ankle. Then she glanced quickly about her—caught up the broom with which she had been sweeping—clasped it tight, and cried:

"Broom, broom, carry me to the house where my sister is locked up!"

The broom bucked and reared angrily, like an unbroken colt. It was only a common house broom, not used to such commands. For a moment Cinnamon was afraid that it would jump right out of her hands. Quickly she smeared another fingerful of green ointment on the broom, stuffed the pot back into her pinafore pocket, and ordered again: "Broom, broom, take me to the house where my sister is a prisoner."

Sulkily, with many jibs and jolts, the broom rose in the air and flew off, while Cinnamon clung to it like a grasshopper to a blade of grass.

At this moment the witch managed to struggle out of the trash basket. Her newspaper hat had come off, her cloak was torn, and her skirt was smeared with squashed banana. She was in a passion. Furiously waving her umbrella, she yelled. "After her! After her! Up the chimney down!"

Obediently the umbrella soared upwards after Cinnamon, while the witch clung to its handle.

But what was happening to Celery, meanwhile?

She had carefully mixed the magic brew, boiling leek and garlic and fennel and hemlock—then she had added moss and green ginger, and pounded all together with a pestle. Then she poured in the rum and powdered gum.

"Now what should I do?" she wondered.

"Find the witch's spare umbrella," the flying fish told her, putting its head out of the fountain.

Celery was nearly startled out of her wits, for the fish had never spoken before. But she answered, "The witch doesn't have a spare umbrella."

"In that case you had better break the aerial off the television set."

The TV set had been one specially ordered for the Rajah of Kichindishpan. The witch never used it. It was made of solid gold, encrusted with diamonds. Celery had a difficult time wrenching off the aerial, for her hands were sticky with fright and ointment, trembling with haste and anxiety.

At last she had it off.

"Now smear yourself with ointment," said the flying fish.

She did so.

"Now say the spell," the flying fish told her.

"How do you know all these things?" asked Celery.

"Because I am a prince. She changed me into a flying fish."

"Then shan't I take you along too?"

"Yes, please!"

So Celery filled a plastic bag with water, and the flying fish jumped neatly into it. Holding the water-filled bag with one hand, Celery grasped the aerial with the other, and cried, "Up the chimney down!"

In a trice she grew thin as a ribbon. In a flash she and the flying fish whirled up the chimney, out through the pot, and over the roof.

"Take me to my grandmother's house!" gasped Celery,

with her mouth full of wind, and the TV aerial did a U-turn and flew to Bagel Street where Mrs. Baker's shop was. The street seemed terribly untidy. A trash basket lay on its side, and garbage was strewn along the street from end to end.

But meanwhile, what about Cinnamon?

She, on the broom, had just flown in the reverse direction and landed on the witch's roof. There she stood, wondering which chimney was the entrance to the witch's room. There were dozens.

"Which is the right chimney?" she asked her broom. But it ducked its head sulkily and refused to answer.

The next moment Mrs. McMurk arrived, her crossed eyes blazing, her newspaper clothes crackling, and her green hair flying out behind her like onion leaves.

She grabbed poor Cinnamon by the scruff of the neck.

"*Now* I've got you, sssslave! You thought you could escape, you little snivelling, sneaking scallywag! Well you shan't have another chance, for I'll eat you on toast!"

And Mrs. McMurk was just about to plunge down the chimney with Cinnamon, when a whole committee of winds arrived, north, south, south-west, north-east, a monsoon, a zephyr, a mistral, a sirocco, a simoon, a typhoon, a harmattan, two trade winds, and a blizzard.

"Leave the child alone!" they all shouted.

The typhoon then spun the witch around a dozen times, and snatched the umbrella from her hand. All the magic ointment was blown off her, so fast did she spin.

She began to grow fatter and fatter and fatter.

"Give me back my umbrella!" she yelled, but the winds took no notice of that. They picked her up and stuffed her headfirst down her own chimney. But by now she was so fat that she stuck halfway down.

Meanwhile the winds had kindly, carefully, gently delicately picked up little Cinnamon and her sulky broom. Carefully, gently, delicately, lovingly, they carried her back to Bagel Street.

"Oh, but my sister, my sister!" she lamented.

"Don't worry," the winds told her, "your sister is safe and sound."

What had happened to Celery?

When she landed in Bagel Street, with the water-filled bag and the television aerial, the first person she saw was her own grandmother, Mrs. Baker, who had stepped outside to see if the winds were ready for their cakes.

"Merciful monsoons!" exclaimed Mrs. Baker in horror. "Just look at all this mess! And only five minutes ago it was all nice and tidy! What in the name of wonder have you been up to, child? Put down that blessed fish and get to work as fast as you can—the winds will be here any minute!"

She was so upset and put about that she never noticed she was speaking to Celery, not Cinnamon.

"Yes, Grandmamma," said Celery. "But I shall need a broom. And can you put this fish in the bath, please? He's really a prince in disguise."

"Broom?" said her grandmother. "But where's the broom you were using? *Prince in disguise*—have you gone clean stark staring—?"

At this moment Nutmeg, hearing all the commotion, put her white-capped head out of the bakery's door. *She* recognized her lost daughter in a single second, and let out a shriek of joy that made all the fire hydrants start spouting water like fountains.

"*Clove!* My own little lost Clove!"

"*Clove?*" said Mrs. Baker, rubbing her eyes. "Have you gone maze-minded? Has everyone lost their wits? That's not Clove, it's Cinnamon."

"It's Clove, it's Clove!"

Luckily, just in time to save a lot of argument, the friendly winds dropped Cinnamon beside her sister in the street.

My word, then, wasn't there a lot of laughing and kissing and crying for joy as the two sisters ran to each other like two drops of rain on the pane! And Clove's mother and grandmother took turns to snatch and hug her, sometimes hugging Cinnamon by mistake, because the sisters were so alike, and sometimes on purpose, because they were so pleased to have the two together again. Mrs. Baker dropped the flying fish in her excitement but luckily he fell into the witch's umbrella, which had been thrown down by the winds, had landed open and upside down, and was now filled with water from the spouting fire hydrants, so that it had lost all its magic.

The first person to pull herself together was old Mrs. Baker.

"Quick, it's nearly the winds' tea time!" said she. "We have only two minutes to clear the street!"

But, as usual, there were lots of people waiting in line at the baker's shop door, in case there were any cakes left over from the winds' tea. They had been pleased to see the family reunion, and were only too glad to help. In ninety-five seconds, with all the helpers, and the water from the fire hydrants, Bagel Street was the cleanest place in the city. Promptly at four o'clock Mrs. Baker tossed up all her cakes to the hovering winds, who joyfully received them. There were just enough cakes left over for the people who had helped clean the street. And up above the winds were purring in the sky like pampered cats.

"We are very, very happy for you," whispered a zephyr breeze, hovering by Cinnamon's cheek. "Is there anything else we can do for you?"

"No, no, not a thing, not a single thing!" joyously cried Cinnamon, hanging on to her sister's hand as if she would never again let it go. But Clove, in the same breath, cried, "Yes, yes, there is! The poor flying fish. Change him back into a prince!"

"Easy!" roared the typhoon, and spun the umbrella round so fast that it became a dizzy blur and vanished entirely. Next moment, out of the blur stepped a handsome prince. But the umbrella had gone for good.

So the prince (in due course) married Clove, and Cinnamon married one of the friendly breezes, who had such an obliging nature that he would carry her wherever she wanted to go, all over the world. And, after Mrs. Baker and her daughter Nutmeg had retired, the two sisters and their husbands looked after the baker's shop.

What about Mrs. McMurk? So far as is known, she is still stuck fast in the chimney. But perhaps by now she has managed to struggle down, back into her room full of treasures. She can't get out, for she has no umbrella and no ointment, so there she must stay.

And all the time the traffic down below goes to and fro, to and fro, to and fro. . . .

Christmas at Troy

The thing that I am going to tell you happened over a hundred years ago—long before such things as cars, radio, or TV had been invented. There were no refrigerators or vacuum cleaners then—there was no electricity. Or, at least, no doubt the electricity was there, fidgeting around in the sky and the ground and in metals and so forth— but people hadn't discovered it yet. They didn't know that the air was full of radio waves and light waves, waiting to be trapped and lined up and passed through radio receivers and on to television screens.

But perhaps people could feel and see things then that we can't see now.

In those days there was a big house called Troy that stood in a wide rolling park full of ancient trees in the county of Kent. A large happy family lived in this house at the time I am telling of—mother, father, and eight or nine children. They were rich, they had dozens of servants—butler, footman, maids, cooks, gardeners, coachmen, carpenters, grooms, housekeeper, librarian, tutors and governesses for the children. The house was like a small world; no need to go outside it. There were cottages for the servants, stables for the horses—there was even a blacksmith, who kept busy attending to all the coach and riding horses as they cast their shoes. There was a moat around the house, and fish in it. There were several nurseries and schoolrooms for the children, and when the carpenters on the estate had a bit of spare time, they used it in making toys—seesaws, swings, rocking horses, dolls' houses.

Everybody was busy and happy. Only once a year was it necessary to call in help from outside. This was when the chimneys needed sweeping, which was usually done during the weeek before Christmas—because at Christmas, of course, people want huge blazing fires in every fireplace, logs piled high and crackling almost up to the mantelpiece—and, naturally, the last thing anybody would wish is a chimney fire at that time, so: get rid of the soot, sweep it away! Besides, soot is good for the slugs in the garden, or rather, bad for them, they detest it; so, a week before Christmas the head gardener of Troy reminded the steward that the slugs were nibbling lacy holes in his winter cabbages; and the steward sent for the sweep, Joshua Clinker, and he came at once, riding through the white frosty park on his donkey with the brushes strapped behind the saddle, while the chimney boy, Matthew, walked after him carrying the sacks.

One of the smallest girls in the family, Eliza, who was

only three, happened to look out of the nursery window, and she let out a shriek.

"Lucy, Loo, hold me tight! There's goblins walking through the park!"

"Those aren't goblins, silly," said her elder sister. "That's the sweep and his boy."

"But they're all black and dreadful!"

"That's because of the soot."

True enough, Mr. Clinker, a bachelor, was black all over. He never bothered to wash, except of a Saturday evening when he visited the public bath, put on his best jacket, and got drunk at the pub; while his boy Matt never washed at all. Hadn't washed in the whole of his life. For a start they lived in a sooty hovel where there was no tap. If you wanted a drink you carried a jug to the pump at the end of the lane. And, in any case, what's the use of washing off the soot at night when you are only going to be covered all over with it again next day? Besides, cold water from the pump is not much use for washing off soot, which is greasy and clings.

Furthermore, Joshua Clinker said that soot was healthy and kept off the fleas.

Matt had never been to school, couldn't read or write, and he didn't know much about anything except soot and chimneys, apart from the things he thought inside his head.

He detested soot, because it was so black. Therefore, he thought, there must, somewhere, be a place where nothing was black, where all the colors were bright and clear. In that place, he thought, would be warm rivers, where you could swim and wash away the soot; there would be wild strawberries bigger than plums, and wild horses gentle as sheep that would let you climb on their backs and ride them. There would be his mother and father too, and his sister. Matt's mother had died when he was six, three years ago, and his dad two years later; Matt and his sister Sue had been sent to the workhouse, and he hadn't seen Sue since she went away to be a scullery maid, but someone told him she had died of the cholera. Anyway, in that place, all three of his family would be with Matt again; and, as well, perhaps, an invisible friend of his called Greg who sometimes came and talked to Matt inside his head. Greg could be very unkind and teasing; Matt wasn't sure if he wanted him in the beautiful place; Greg was a bad friend, not a good friend. Still, here and at the moment, a teasing invisible friend was better than no friend at all.

These were the thoughts that occupied Matt as he and his master approached the house of Troy through the big frosty park. Matt's hard bare feet made no sound on the frozen rutted track; all that could be heard was the sound of the donkey's hoofs clopping along, and Mr. Clinker sometimes growling, "Giddap, there!"

Troy was a huge mansion. People said there was a room in it for every day in the year: 365 altogether. But no one in the family had ever managed to count all the rooms. Sometimes one of the children started to do so—

but there always came an interruption before they were finished. From a distance the house looked like a small town.

"Is that all really just one house?" Matt would have liked to ask, but he knew his master would only cuff him, so he kept quiet.

They crossed the bridge over the moat, which was frozen. Matt looked down at the dark gray ice, powdered with wriggly patterns, and wondered if the fish were all right in under there.

They went through an arch into a huge frosty court-yard, big as the main square of a market town, didn't stop there, but passed through another arch into a smaller courtyard and then into a third, smaller yet, this one paved with cobblestones. Here they were met by a foot-man, who took them to the Great Hall, where they were to start work. Everywhere along the passages ahead of them old sheets had been spread over the flagstones, so it was easy to see where they were meant to go.

Mr. Clinker had been to Troy many times before, but this was Matt's first visit.

"Got a new boy, I see, then, Mr. Clinker, since last year?" observed the footman, who wore a striped apron and black breeches and striped stockings and buckled shoes.

"That's right," grunted Joshua Clinker. "Lost one here last year."

"Oh, ah, yes, so you did—Well, this is where you

start. You know the regular order, I daresay."

"Oughta know it by now," grunted Mr. Clinker. "Been here a mort o' times."

And he began fitting brushes together.

"Up you goo, boy, fust off," he said.

Matt had begun to tremble when they reached the Great Hall. He always did at this stage. That was why, walking across the park, he had tried so hard to think about other things. He did know, though, that, once he was inside the chimney, it wouldn't be so bad as he feared—or not quite; it was just the thought beforehand that was so terrible.

"Up you goo, boy!" repeated Mr. Clinker impatiently.

So Matt gulped, ducked his head under the high stone chimneypiece, stepped nervously with his bare feet in the warm ashes—not *too* warm, thank goodness, they'd had the kindness to let the fire out overnight—stuck his toes and fingers into the cracks between the bricks, and began to climb.

"This 'un be straight up!" Mr. Clinker shouted after him. "There's others in Troy as be trickier, but this 'ere feller's plain as a pikestaff." And he reached up under the mantel and passed a handbrush to his boy.

In the days before vacuum cleaners, that was how chimneys were swept; boys had to climb up inside them, and rub or scrape off the soot that had collected, as they climbed. Men, of course, were too big for the job, it had to be boys. Nobody thought this odd; people go down mines, so why not up chimneys? If the boys were slow and awkward, or got themselves stuck in tight places, some chimney sweeps lit a handful of paper or shavings in the fireplace down below, to hurry them up.

Matt was encouraged to discover that the chimney in the Great Hall at Troy was so very wide that there was no possibility of his getting stuck—which was what he dreaded most; in fact a flight of brick steps had been let into the side of the chimney shaft, going round and round, a kind of circular staircase, so that it was not at all difficult to climb. And the bricks were not too hot for his bare feet. Up he went nimbly, sweeping as he went, dislodging showers of soot, and soon he could hear the jabbering of starlings and see light above; before long he was able to stick his head right out of the enormous decorated chimney pot and look all over the roofs of Troy. What a sight that was! There were enough gables, ledges, peaks, towers, weathercocks, pinnacles, domes, dormers, and gargoyles for a whole city. And all covered thick with white frost. Beyond the roofs lay the park of Troy, with its massive oak and chestnut trees, and far away Matt could see herds of thin spidery fallow deer snuffing for chestnuts in the winter grass.

"You get to the top, boy?" bawled Mr. Clinker down below.

"Yes, Master . . ."

"Then make haste down with 'ee! We got another forty-nine chimbleys to sweep yet. And winter days 'on't last long."

Reluctantly, Matt began going down backward. That

part was always much worse. Climbing up, you could see the light above, if you were lucky; it shone down and showed you where to grip with your fingers; but the descent was trickier. The soot you had loosened on your way up fell down in choking clouds and half suffocated you; sometimes you fell too, and scraped your elbows and thighs; or your clothes caught and tore on nails and sharp splinters of stone. Some masters sent their boys up naked, but Mr. Clinker allowed Matt to wear cotton breeches, in case he came out somewhere unexpected. For many of the chimneys in Troy connected together like roads leading to a town; you might climb up one and accidentally come down another, into a different room from the one where you started.

"They never did find that boy o' mine, Greg, what got lost last winter?" Mr. Clinker inquired of the footman as they waited for Matt to scramble his way down.

"Not as I ever heard on; there's a regular miz-maze of chimneys at Troy; it'd take Prince Christodore Columbus seven years wi' a silken clue to work his way through all on 'em. Likely the poor liddle varmint is still in there, some'eres, shriveled up 'an toasted to a crispet."

Neither man looked particularly bothered. This seemed an everyday affair to them. Boys did get lost in chimneys. By and by Matt dropped down into the hearth, sneezing and coughing; Mr. Clinker screwed his long brushes together and poked them up to dislodge any final flakes or lumps of soot; then all that had come down was swept up into sacks, and they moved on to other rooms, other chimneys.

By mid-afternoon, when the early winter twilight had begun to close down, Matt was very tired. He had climbed chimney after chimney, so many that he had lost count. There had been no pauses to rest. And some of the chimneys were by no means so easy as the big circle-stepped one in the Great Hall; some were narrow and crooked, went sideways or slantways, or joined confusingly with other chimneys. Once Matt fell, hurting himself quite badly, and came out in the housekeeper's parlor; she slapped him, called him a careless little noddy, and told him to get back up the chimney directly. Once he got himself scorched, venturing too near the kitchen chimneys, which still had fires down below, for the cooks were hard at work making Christmas cakes and pies.

Matt knew little about Christmas; his family had been too poor to celebrate the festival, except by a day off work. Which just meant less money that week.

As the afternoon dwindled, the guiding patch of sky up at the top of the chimneys turned pale green, then dark blue, then black. Groping about in the hot, sooty, bricky dark, Matt longed to hear the voice of his master calling, "Come down, Matt, boy. That'll hatta do for today."

But Matt did not hear Mr. Clinker's voice. What he did hear—first as a distant whisper, then closer—was the voice of his friend Greg, his teasing, invisible half-friend.

"Matt! Hey, Matt! Hey, Matty boy! Come thisaway an' I'll show ye a wondrous nice place!"

Once or twice before Greg had led Matt into bad trouble with his suggestions: once he persuaded Matt to jump down from a high ledge, which was a terrible mistake; once he promised to wake him and did not; once he dared Matt to ride Bet, the donkey, which earned him a hard beating from Mr. Clinker; so this time Matt was wary.

"What manner o' nice place? I dassn't tarry, Greg, or I'll get lost in these dark old chimneys; and when I do get out master'll tan me."

"Oh, but a real purty spot it be! Where the sun do shine, and there's all the folks ye lost, and the berries grows right outa the snow—big and red they be as pullets' eggses. . . ."

Matt was terribly tempted. He had been in the dark for so long that he felt sure he was lost anyway, in this crisscross of chimneys—he was so tired he had almost forgotten which was up and which was down—and, from the direction where Greg's voice seemed to whisper, he could fancy that he saw a twinkle of light. Staring, peering, straining his eyes in the hot sooty dark, he seemed to be able to see, as if through a pinhole, a tiny village, all covered in tinselly snow, with holly trees and people tumbling and laughing—his father and Sue his sister— and were there not, yes, there were, big glistening red strawberries, growing right there in the white powdery snow! And not a pinch of dark, not a whisker of dark anywhere.

"Well, mebbe, Greg, I'll come for jist a look—"he started to say, feeling with his grimy and bleeding fingers for a good handhold. Then something sharply pinched one of his fingers—ouch! What was that? Matt flinched back, wondering if it could be a rat that had bitten him— rats often did live in chimneys. But, feeling with the other hand, he discovered that what gripped his finger was a thin loop of metal, something like a ring, only it did not seem to go all the way around. It gripped his finger but there was a gap.

"Maybe 'tis valuable," he thought to himself. "Maybe owd Mus' Clinker'll be pleased when he sees it."

Just then he heard old Mus' Clinker's voice furiously shouting from far down below.

"You there, you boy! If you baint down afore I counts ten I'll give ye sich a leathering, ye'll need to eat your dinner standing for a week. Only, ye won't *get* no dinner, I be telling 'ee!"

"Yes, master, yes, I'm-a-coming," called Matt, and began hastily scrambling, sliding, tumbling himself down all anyhow, hurting his elbows and shins on all kinds of rough lumps and corners. Mr. Clinker's voice had seemed to come from a great distance away. In his hurry Matt crawled recklessly down a slanting tunnel that seemed to turn in the right direction—became stuck—struggled in a frenzy of panic, pushed, kicked with his feet and thrust ahead with his hands. Suddenly a great warm piece of masonry gave way entirely under his urgent pressure, and fell. Matt plummeted after it, landing on his head.

He saw sparks, and then darkness, and that was all he remembered for a long, long time.

When he came to himself again he found that he was still lying in darkness. The smell of hot soot, sharp and dusty, was all around him. Matt cried a little. This was his worst nightmare. He knew that he was not at home in Mr. Clinker's hut; firstly, because it was warm; secondly, because there was no sound of snoring. Now he began to remember odd remarks he had overheard, among Mr. Clinker and his friends. "Troy, eh? Lucky if you don't lose him—" with a sideways nod toward Matt. "I've heard tell as how there's more boys mislaid in they chimbleys than cherries in owd Mus' Bowden's orchard." And Clinker's grunted reply, "What's a boy more or less? Boys is easy come by."

Lost in the chimneys of Troy! How would he ever find his way out?

Matt called feebly, "Help! *Help!*" But his voice seemed deadened by the masses of heavy soot that lay and dangled all around him. He dared not call too loud, in case the soot cascaded down in a fearful avalanche and smothered him.

Where in the world could he be? Somewhere out of sight, out of mind entirely, hidden in the huge depths of Troy.

"But I won't be lost, I *won't* be," thought Matt. "'Twas all that mischievous Greg's fault. I'll never listen to him again, never. If he hadn't called me—if I hadn't turned aside after him—"

He began to wriggle carefully along on his stomach, pushing up a great wave of soot ahead of him. And it was as well that he took such care, for, after ten minutes of crawling, he felt the floor beneath him come to a stop and found his head and shoulders extending outwards over nothing.

Used to chimneys, Matt was not daunted by this. There was a shaft going down: good. All he had to do now was somehow reverse himself, let his legs over the edge first, and so make his descent. Easier said than done, though, in the narrow tunnel through which he had been crawling, for it fitted him as tightly as a glove. But the only alternative was to push out and fall headfirst. He was very anxious not to do *that* again.

Still hesitating there, half stuck, like a mouse emerging from its hole, Matt was startled to hear a faint faraway sound of bells jingling. "That be right rummy," he thought. "I wonder what time o'day 'tis? Could it be the servants' dinner bell? Or the lesson bell for all they children?"

The whole huge house was completely silent about him. Somehow it felt later than that. Not like bell time. It felt like the middle of a tremendously long night. Matt waited, trying not to breathe too loud, hoping that the sound would come again, so that he could gauge its direction.

It did come again. And this time from straight above him. Looking up, Matt was first startled and then delighted to see a star. A real star! Just one, fitted, he supposed, in the center of a chimney pot. He stared at it yearningly, wistfully, upraised on his tired hands.

Next moment, to his sorrow, the star vanished, blotted out as if a cloud had covered it. But then, suddenly, it reappeared, and the sound of jingling grew louder, as if dozens of tiny muffin men, with their bells, were invading the chimneys of Troy.

And then Matt fairly gasped. For he beheld such a sight as he had never in his life seen before, and almost certainly never would again. Down around the wide chimney, lippety-lippety (and now he knew where he must be, in the Great Hall shaft, with its circular brick stair) down the brick steps, round and round, lower and lower, came a tiny shining procession, a sleigh drawn by twelve luminously glowing reindeer about the size of squirrels. They made their own radiance as they descended, dropping neatly from step to step, half gliding, half flying, while the driver held the reins with a light hand, as if he trusted his team, and paid more attention to making certain that none of the load was jolted out of his sled, which, like a carrier's cart, was piled high with tidy, minute bundles, all tied with glistening ribbon. The small caped driver had a long white beard, and his head was aureoled with light.

"Eh!" Matt gave a long sigh of wonder. "He must be one o' the little folk, surelye!" Matt had heard tell of them, long ago, when he was a child.

Although startled to death, and somewhat scared at the sight of this mysterious little bright vehicle making its quiet jingling way down the winding brick stair (one of the reindeer, he observed, was trotting a bit lame, favoring its off fore), Matt was not going to waste the chance of the dim glow they gave out in the chimney. When they were below him, but still visible, he managed to wriggle and thrust himself forward, grab hold of two brick steps, and then cleverly swing and push himself sideways until he knelt on one step and grasped another. After that, of course, it was easy enough to swivel round and scramble down, lippety-lippety, just as the shining team had done, and so reach the high arched fireplace of the Great Hall. A new fire had been laid here but not lit, piled across the great firedogs shaped like dragons. Matt skirted it, careful not to dislodge the dry sticks.

By now he was fairly certain that he must have dreamed his amazing vision. A tiny sleigh, drawn by shining reindeer smaller than rabbits! Impossible! Even Greg would laugh at that!

But no; when Matt crept out, on legs that shook with tiredness, there they still were! The team had been pulled up on the warm flagstones of the Great Hall, and stood tossing their glittering heads; the driver had alighted from the sleigh and seemed to be searching for something.

What could he be seeking?

Matt glanced about the big shadowy room, which was lit only by one high lamp in a red glass shade, and he sighed with wonder.

This morning or—whenever he had seen the room first, perhaps longer ago than that?—the big chamber had been empty and bare, stripped of its furniture, ready for the sweep's sooty activities. But now the furniture had been brought back, a long table with twenty chairs round it, and a sideboard. The table was laid for a meal, with a smooth white cloth, and twinkling glass, gleaming china, shining silver spoons and forks. A great posy of flowers was in the middle and twenty crisp white linen napkins folded into the shape of roses. On the sideboard were shallow bowls filled with different fruits, and candles in cut-glass candlesticks, and more sprays of flowers. In one dim corner of the room there seemed to be growing a tree—a fifteen-foot fir tree—adorned with strands of dripping, glistening tinsel and a hundred silver balls. There were sugarplums on the tree too, and peppermint candy canes striped in red and white.

Along under the mantelpiece, Matt noticed, hung about a dozen stockings—all sizes from a gigantic one at the far end to a tiny striped sock above him; each sock seemed to be filled with knobby contents, and each had a sprig of holly sticking out of the top.

Under the fir tree lay wrapped packages. And on either side of it were other things: a rocking horse painted in brilliant red and white with a red leather saddle; a dolls' house, with the front swung open to show the furnished interior; also tops, hoops, bats, balls, kites, skates, boats.

Matt had never owned any toys. Half these things were a puzzle to him; he did not know their use. But he thought they were beautiful. Just the same, they did not attract him half as much as the small, glimmering sleigh and its bearded, caped driver, who was now striding briskly about, back and forth, in front of the fireplace, carefully inspecting the flagstone floor and the cracks between the hearthstones.

"For it must have been here or hereabouts," the driver muttered to himself. "Not ten minutes out on our journey but I noticed that March had begun to dot-and-go-one. Hey, my beauties! January!—February!—August, May, September!—look about, use your eyes! Help your poor old master! Where did it fall? Where can it have rolled to? Where, by holly and mistletoe, can it be?"

"What is it, sir?" asked Matt, stepping forward out of the shadows of the hearth. "What have you lost?"

The little driver spun round and stared at Matt alertly.

"Heyday! Whom have we here? Who hearkens to the chimes of midnight? Who sees the months float by? Who watches while all others slumber? Eh?"

"My name is Matt, sir," the boy said, rather timidly.

"Well, Matt, well met! How is it that you, of all humankind, can see us?"

"I don't know, sir."

"Do you know who I am?"

"N-no, sir." Unless, Matt thought, the tiny driver was the Lord of Troy. But that seemed most unlikely. Lords do not generally enter their houses by the chimney at dead of night. Nor are they so small.

"My name is Nicholas, child, have you never heard it?"

"Oh, yes," said Matt, "there was a young 'un over at the work'us called Nicholas; Nick we used to call him for short. But he took the cholera and died."

The driver sighed. "Well," he said after a moment, "some call me Nick for short also. And some call me Klaus. But if you have never heard of me, my boy, I still wonder that you are able to see me so clearly."

"Perhaps it is because I fell on my head in the chimney, sir?"

"Perhaps!" the driver said with a dry chuckle. "And pity 'tis, if so! Would that the whole world might fall on its head."

"But sir—" Matt gathered a little courage, as the driver seemed so friendly, and the reindeer turned to look at him with gentle curious eyes that shone like moonlit dewdrops. "Are you one o' the pisky folk, sir? And what is it that you have lost?"

"Pisky folk?" The driver laughed. "No—but they are my young cousins. As to what I have lost—never before has Flying Nick been obliged to turn back—but, by some secret quirk of Destiny, one of my prancers there, mad March, the white one with ivory antlers—March cast a shoe—did you not, my pretty?—and was running lame as a one-winged crow. So back on our tracks we were obliged to turn. Not a dwelling in the whole spinning globe has ever had *two* visits from me on Christmas night before, but only this old Troy . . ."

"Cast a shoe? Why, what would it look like, sir?"

"Easy answered! Just turn up your near fore, lightfoot May, my beauty, and give the gentleman, our friend Matt here, a sight of your pretty shoe!"

Not only May, but all twelve reindeer politely curled up a hoof, back or fore, and displayed to Matt their elegant tiny silver shoes, no bigger than the circle of a thimble.

And then Matt remembered what he had around his finger.

"Why, sir—why—perhaps it is this—could it be this?"

Trying to pull the circle off his pitch-black finger he rubbed it, and saw the glint of silver.

"By the crown of the forest! There it is! No wonder, boy, that you can see us so plain! And I am mighty obliged to you, indeed. For that you shall have as reward whatever you care to name. And Nick is not one to stint on gifts— eh, January? Eh, my frisky June?"

Solemnly, the reindeer nodded their antlered heads up and down.

"Reward?" Matt shook his head, still tugging at the tiny circlet. "I want nothing, sir. Or naught that you can give me. Not any *thing*," he added, trying to explain.

"Heyso? How can that be? All that's in the snowy globe is yours for the asking, child."

And the little driver gestured a circle with his hands in which, just for a moment, Matt seemed to see lands, oceans, flowers, forests, mountains, treasures—then it was gone again.

"But all I do want, sir—my friend Greg seemed to promise it an hour ago—" Was it merely an hour? Or had it been an endless, lifelong stretch of dark time? "My friend Greg seemed to say that he could take me *there*."

"*There*? And where, my dear boy, is *There*?"

"Where the strawberries grow out of the snow, sir. And where my mam is, and my dad, and my little sister Sue that went for a cookmaid. And where there's laughing and singing all day, and no dark at all."

"Ah, *There*! Now I do understand. But—" Nick smiled and sighed. "*There*, dear boy, is not for you, just yet. No, not yet. There's tasks for you in store yet—fruits to pick, boxes to open, hills to climb, books to read. All in time's good grace you will find your way to There."

"Will I so, sir? Truly?"

"Without a lie. On the word of Nick." The driver touched the ring of light that encircled his head. "But now—in the meantime—I can do for you one of two things. And you must choose. If you wish, I can make you free of all this—"

He waved a hand at the hushed, waiting hall, with its gifts, its fragrant tree, its shaded light, the glitter of its spread table.

"I can make you a part of Troy, I can put you in the midst of it, as if you had belonged to it from birth. Which, indeed, you would have. The youngest son of Troy."

Matt looked about him. He was deeply tempted. Belong to all this! Be a part of it! Never to sweep a chimney again. Never to taste soot, smell soot, fall in darkness with bruised elbows and skinned knees. Never to be afraid.

But he took a second breath, and said, "Or, sir? You said you could do one of two things. What is the other, if you please?"

Nick laughed jovially. "There's my canny boy! There's my cagey boy! Always look at the other side. Beat about the bush—even about the holly bush! Why, child, the other choice would be to skip into the sleigh and come along with me!"

"Where would you go, sir?" Matt asked, his eyes already beginning to shine.

"Why, first to the blacksmith, old Charley Wayland, ancient Vulcan, who lives over the cloudcaps, in the thunder mountains. First we must call on him to have March's shoe nailed on right and tight. Where then? Every single where. Not a village is missed out, not a house, not a hearth. But, after that—"

"What after that, sir?"

"Then, after the ride, I must toss you out into the cold old world to make your way by yourself as best you can with what knowledge you have picked up along the way. In the end the ride is bound to finish."

"Oh, but sir, I wouldn't mind *that*!" cried Matt. "If I could ride with you—even for a short way—I wouldn't ask anything better, anything more!"

"Is that your choice! Brave boy! Step on board, then!"

And, whether Matt grew smaller or the sleigh grew bigger, he could not have said, but the next moment they were whirling up the chimney, round and round, shining like a puff of smoke with sparks in it, Nick holding the reins, Matt still with the silver reindeer shoe on his finger. For it had shrunk with him and still remained firmly clasped.

"Indeed, sir," he said, "I don't think I'd have been able to get if off."

"Old Wayland will be able to do that, never fear," his companion said. "But that makes me certain—as indeed I was from the beginning—that you were destined to come along with me. So, what you see on this ride— what you learn—remember well! Put it to good use!"

"Oh, I will, sir—I will!" Matt promised, clinging to the front rail of the sleigh, as the frosty landscape unrolled below them and the stars flashed past in bundles.

"Perhaps you will find out something new for those sleeping down there—who knows? At all events," Nick said, laughing again, "it is lucky I met you, for otherwise, with March so lame, I should have fallen late, and later, on all my visits. Half the world would not have had its Christmas until February. And that would never do!"

Matt laughed too, he hardly understood why; and the reindeer shook their jingling bells, and the sleigh flew on through the brilliant night.

The Midnight Rose

There's a village called Wish Wintergreen in the county
of Somerset, just where the Mendip hills slide down into
the marshes. Not a large village—only forty houses, or
thereabouts, set round in a square, but with all that's
needed—one church, one pub, one school, bank, butcher,
baker, builder, plumber (who also does TV repairs),
chemist, jail, fish and chip shop, courthouse, post office;
outside the square of houses, and their long green gardens
full of apple trees and roses and cabbages, there are eighty-
nine green mounds, set round in a ring. How big are the
mounds? About as high as a double-decker bus. The
children roll down them in summertime, and toboggan
down them in winter. What's under them? Nobody knows.
Canon Godliman, grandfather to the present vicar, started
digging into one of them a hundred years ago; he was
struck dumb for a month; then he couldn't stop talking,
night or day, for another month. His wife couldn't decide
which was worse. What did he talk about? All kinds of

queer things—unicorn teams, the city of Neksheb, the evil spirit of the north who plays his gloomy strains in Swedish waters, the three frivolous battles of Britain, Roman soldiers who carried bundles of nettles to keep them warm, Doll money, and the wake of Teanley Night. No one could make head or tail of such stuff. At the end of the second month he died, worn out; but he was eighty-nine, so it might have happened anyway.

One day, in the gloomy month of January, this tale begins. The village was very quiet that day. Wish Wintergreen is a quiet place at all times, the natives don't talk a lot, but that day it was extra quiet. Christmas had long gone by, but spring was nowhere yet in sight. Not a soul in the road or on the green. In the village school the teacher, Miss Clerihand, was saying: "Well, children. We all know what's going on in the courthouse today, and we can't help thinking about it. So there's no use trying to do sums or spelling. We'll do history instead. Barbie, where was the land of Dilmun?"

"On the edge of the world, miss."

"What was there, Paul?"

"A beautiful garden, with cucumbers and apples and grapes in it."

"What else, Sammy?"

"In that garden, the raven utters no cry,
The lion kills not."

"What else, Tom?"

"In that garden, the wolf snatches not the lamb,
The sick man says not 'I am sick.' "

"What else, Ted?"

"In that garden the old woman says not
'I am an old woman,'
The old man says not 'I am an old man.' "

"Who lived there, Cecily?"

"Our great-grandmother Eve."

"What was her other name, Harold?"

"Ninmu, the lady who makes green things grow."

"Who came to the land of Dilmun, Ellen?"

"A gypsy, one of the wandering tribe of the Tchingani."

"His name, Sarah?"

"Duke Michael."

"What did he do, Paul?"

"Told the lady Eve's fortune. Said she would have two beautiful babies."

"What did she give him, Chris?"

"A basket of earth with a root in it."

"Where did he go, Sammy?"

"In a boat, down one of the four rivers flowing out of the land of Dilmun."

"And where then, Tom?"

"Half around the world to Somerset, the Land of Summer."

"What did he do there, Barbie?"

"Built himself an island and planted a garden."

"And in the middle of it," chorused all the children, "he put the basket of earth and the root."

"What happened then?"

"He grew old and died."

"What did he say before he died?"

"Ten thousand years from today, on a night midway between winter and spring, the rose shall blossom at midnight," all the children said.

"Who will be there to behold it?"

"Whoever is there to behold it, they shall remember the beginnings of the world, and shall also see forward to the ending of the world. And in their power shall it be to make that ending a ruin or a victory."

"Good," said Miss Clerihand. "What became of Dilmun, Sammy?"

"It was swept away in the Great Flood."

"Where to, Tom?"

"It floated off into space."

"Where is it now, Barbie?"

"Became one of Saturn's moons."

"Right. And when is the night that the rose shall blossom?"

"Between now and St. Valentine's Day!" they all shouted.

"And where will it blossom?"

"Here! Right here! In our own village."

"Right," said Miss Clerihand again. "And we don't want any strangers coming here to dig up the rose and take it away to the Science Museum or the Natural History Museum, do we?"

"No, *that* we don't!"

"Good," said the teacher once more. "You know your history well. I think we'll take a break now and play Up

Jenkins. Joe," she said to one boy, who had not answered any of the questions, but sat quiet and pale in the back row, "Joe, you may go outside if you like, for a breath of air."

Joe nodded without reply, slid from his seat, put on his duffel jacket, and ran outside. His face was marked by the tracks of two tears which had rolled down in spite of all his efforts to keep them in.

When he left the classroom, Joe walked out of the school porch and crossed the village green, where a great dead elm stood and a new young oak had been planted. He stood listening outside the gray stone courthouse, where some cars were parked. No sound came from inside, and he did not dare go in. So instead he walked very slowly, kicking the frosty ground, to the high-arched bridge over the Wintergreen brook, which ran very clear, deep, and rapid here, over white pebbles, with watercress growing in clumps.

Joe sat on the parapet of the bridge, his shoulders hunched, his face downcast, chewing on a stem of watercress and listening to the silence.

Presently, along rolled a Landrover, which looked as if it had been driven over mountains and through deserts and maybe through the Red Sea as well—every inch of it was rusty, there were shreds of palm leaves and coconut fiber and seals' whiskers sticking out of the cracks, and in the dust on panels and windscreen rude remarks had been scrawled in dozens of foreign languages.

The vehicle slowed to a halt beside Joe and the motor stopped as if it meant never to start again. The driver jumped out.

"Where's everybody?" he asked. He was a tall, bronzed man, with a harsh, beak-nosed face, and sparkling black eyes, and bushy black eyebrows; his hair must have been black once, too, but had turned white as snow, what remained of it; Joe noticed that a curved metal plate had been placed over part of his bald crown. And down his left cheek ran a great dried scar.

"Where's everybody?" he asked again.

"Indoors," said Joe shortly, "watching the trial on TV."

"What trial?"

"The one that's going on in there," Joe jerked his head toward the courthouse.

"Why don't they watch it live?"

"They'd sooner stop at home."

"Who's being tried? And for what?"

Joe paused and swallowed, began to speak and stopped. At last he said, "The man who dug up the trowel."

"What trowel?" The stranger's deep eyes flashed.

But Joe said, "How did your head get hurt, mister?"

"In a fight," answered the man absently, "in the Valley of Gehenna. But a Persian doctor put this silver plate in for me, to replace the missing piece of bone."

"Must be hot when the sun shines on it, mister?"

"Then I wear a hood. The silver plating picks up sounds and echoes very well," said the traveler, tapping his head with the car key which he held; the silver surface gave out a faint ringing sound, like a glass tapped with a fork.

The stranger asked again: "What trowel did the man dig up?"

"An old wooden one. Ten thousand years old, the professor from the London Museum says it is."

"Why should they try a man for digging up a wooden trowel?"

"Because he won't give it to the museum people. He buried it again, just where he found it. And he won't tell them where that is. So they say he'll be sentenced to prison for ten years for disobeying a Court Order and refusing to hand over important historical objects."

"When will the trial end?"

"Today or tomorrow. Or the next day."

"Who is this man?"

Slowly and reluctantly the boy said, "He's my father."

"What's his name?"

"Joe Mathinwell." The boy nodded toward a small builder's yard with a painted sign over the gate: "Joseph Mathinwell, builder, plumber & undertaker."

"Where *did* he dig up the trowel?" asked the traveler inquisitively, but Joe, turning to give him a clear steady look out of slightly red-rimmed eyes, answered, "If he had told me, do you think I would tell *you*?"

"No," said the traveler. "No, I can see that you would not. It is plain that you are a brave, trustworthy boy."

Joe made no reply to that.

The stranger walked across to the shop of Mrs. Honeysett, Baker & Confectioner, went in, and bought a rock cake. The old lady observed that when he put his hand down to the tray with buns in it, the rock cake jumped right up into his hand.

"Do you know," asked the traveler, "whereabouts in this village the Midnight Rose is expected to bloom?"

Mrs. Honeysett shook her head. "Reckon the only fellow who could answer that question is Joe Mathinwell, father of that poor little mite out there. Ah, and his mum dead two years past, of the jaundice, and his dad liable for a ten-year sentence! But I've told Joe I'll keep the lad and look after him, if things fall out according."

The traveler left her shop and went into that of Mr. Chitterley the butcher, where he bought a slice of ham. As he moved toward the cash desk a large china pig that stood above it fell to the floor and was smashed to pieces.

"Can you tell me," asked the stranger, "whereabouts in this village the Midnight Rose will bloom?"

"No, I can't," snapped the butcher, looking with annoyance at his shattered pig. "And if I could, I wouldn't. We can keep a secret in these parts, mister."

The traveler went into the Somerset and West Country bank, where he cashed a traveler's check. As he wrote his name a great looking-glass on the wall behind the counter fell down and cracked clean across. And the big crystal chandelier that hung in the middle of the ceiling let out a faint secret hum, which was echoed, even more faintly, by the silver plate on the traveler's head.

"Can you tell me," he asked, handing in his check, "where the Midnight Rose will bloom?"

"Certainly not," was the manager's short answer, as he counted out pound notes. "This is not the kind of information we are required to divulge to customers. *Good* day to you."

The traveler went on to the chemist, Mr. Powdermaker, where he bought fivepence worth of powdered ginger, to the TV repair shop, fish bar, post office, and to the church (where he looked up rather warily at the stone griffins and dolphins which grinned down at him from the corners of the tower). At each place he asked the same question, and everywhere received the same answer.

The vicar was more polite about it than his parishioners.

"Really, my dear sir, it's impossible to say where Joe Mathinwell might have dug up the trowel. Mr. Mathinwell is such a very busy man. Why, in this past week he has laid two new floorboards in the school, repaired a piece of paving in the south aisle of the church, cleaned out Mrs. Honeysett's drains, unblocked Mr. Chitterley's slaughterhouse outlet, renewed the wiring at the bank, installed damp-proofing in the pub cellars, dug out a cavity for Mr. Powdermaker's new boiler, laid a cement floor in Farmer Fothergill's pigsties, repaired Mr. Porbeagle's basement stairs, and mended a crack in the post office counter. So you see he might have come across the trowel in any one of those places."

"And where he found the trowel, there the rose is, d'you reckon?" eagerly asked the traveler.

The vicar at once began to look extremely absent-minded.

"Ah, well, maybe, maybe, who can say?" he replied guardedly. "I know, myself, when I am gardening, that I tend to drop my tools in all kinds of odd places, not necessarily just where I have been working. But now excuse me, excuse me, my dear sir, I must go and write a sermon this very minute," and he hurried away, his shabby coattails flying.

The traveler ended up at the pub, The Rose Revived, where he was able to obtain a room for the night. But Mrs. Bickerstaff the landlady was not able to give him lunch. "I've my hands that full with cooking a meal for the lawyers and the judge," she explained. "Not but what I wouldn't object to drop a spoonful of arsenic in that old Tartar's Windsor soup! But business is business. I can make you a sandwich, though, sir."

"A sandwich will be enough. How long is the trial expected to continue?"

"Another two—three days, maybe. 'Tis to be hoped as the rose'll bloom before sentence is passed, and then Joe Mathinwell, poor soul, won't need to hold his tongue no longer."

"Do you know where the rose will bloom, Mrs. Bickerstaff?"

"Ah," she replied, "that'd be telling, wouldn't it?"

After he had eaten his sandwich, the stranger went into the courtroom to hear the trial of Joseph Mathinwell

taking its course. But the arguments back and forth between the lawyers were very dull; they seemed to be about
what grounds the government had for considering that it
had a claim to the trowel that Mr. Mathinwell had dug
up, and why Mr. Mathinwell ought to have obeyed the
Court Order to produce the trowel. Nothing about where
he had found it.

Mr. Mathinwell himself sat calm and quiet. He was a
thin pale man with a tussock of darkish hair on the top
of his head. He kept his eyes steadily on his joined hands,
and never looked up at the stranger sitting in the public
benches. The old judge brooded at his high desk: Jeffreys,
his name was, Mrs. Bickerstaff had told the traveler, Lord
Roderick Jeffreys, descended from that same wicked old
Judge Jeffreys who had conducted the Bloody Assizes in
the neighboring county of Dorset; and had the same kind
of reputation, took pride in sentencing offenders to the
maximum penalty. He looked like that too: bitter mouth
shut like a rat trap and deep-sunk eyes like holes out of
which something nasty might suddenly pop.

By the afternoon's end matters were no farther advanced, and the judge stumped out to his Bentley and
had himself driven away to Mendip Magna, where there
was a three-star hotel.

School was over for the day; children were catapulting
from the gray stone building and across the bridge over
the Wintergreen brook; the stranger began asking them
questions.

"Do any of you know where this Midnight Rose is expected to bloom? In the post office, maybe? Or the laundrette?"

Laughing and chattering they surrounded him.

"My dad says it'll be in the British Legion hall!" "No—in Farmer Tillinghast's barn!" "No—down the Youth Club!" "Not there, glue-brain—at the wishing well! You come with me, mister—I'll show you!" "No, mister—you come with *me!*" "With me!" "With me!"

This way and that they dragged him. Deciding that the wishing well sounded the likeliest site, he pulled himself from a dozen hands and followed Cissy Featherstone.

Meanwhile young Joe Mathinwell had been allowed a few words with his father by the kindly Sergeant of the Court, who at other times was Fred Nightingale the sexton.

"Only five minutes, now, mind!"

They were in the front office of the little jail, which had two cells, one for males, one for females. This was the first time in living memory that it had been used.

"Dad!" said young Joe urgently. "There's a stranger in the village and he's asking around everybody and all over for where the rose is going to bloom!"

"Is he a newspaper reporter? Is he offering money?"

"I didn't hear, but he asked Mrs. Honeysett, and Sam Chitterley, and Mr. Moneypenny, and Mr. Powdermaker and Mr. Godliman and lots of others."

"So? Did they tell?" asked Joe's father with a keen look.

"I reckon not. So now he's asking the kids."

"Well," said Mr. Mathinwell, "I reckon they won't tell him either."

"Who d'you think he is, Dad?"

"Oh," said Joe's father wearily, "who can tell? Best take no chances. Maybe he's one o' them scientific foundations wishful to get hold of the rose and *measure* it. Or a film company a-wanting to film it."

"Would that be so wrong, Dad?"

"There's things," said Joe Mathinwell, "ought to be kept private and quiet. Remember what it says in the good book: 'And after the fire, a still, small voice.' Do you think that still small voice would 'a' been heard if there'd been thousands of folk camping and shuffling around, and dozens of TV cameras? 'He that contemneth small things shall fall,' it do say in Ecclesiasticus. Don't *you* do that, Joe."

"No, Dad, but—"

"Time's up, Joe, son," called Fred Nightingale, keeping watch at the street door. "Joe," said his father quickly, "that rose oughta be watered. See to it, will ye?"

"Yes, Dad," said Joe, gulping. "How much water?"

"Not too much. Just a liddle—just as much as it asks for."

The Mathinwell garden had the best roses and the biggest cabbages in Wintergreen; Joseph, his neighbors said, could talk to green things through the tips of his fingers.

"What kind of water, Dad?" said Joe urgently.

But Mr. Nightingale firmly shooed the boy out.

"Mrs. Honeysett taking good care of 'ee?" called Joseph senior with anxious love in his voice.

"Yes, Dad . . ." Then Joe was out on the frosty, twilit green, his eyes brimming with tears, and his mind with worry.

The stranger had now returned from the wishing well, and the various other false goals offered him by the village children (the way to the wishing well had been a particularly long and slippery track along the side of a cowy valley); he was not angry at being fooled, but he looked thoughtful. He began to walk toward Joe, who broke into a desperate scamper, nipped through Mrs. Honeysett's side gate, along to the back of her garden between the bee hives, through Mr. Porbeagle's allotment, and so out among the great grassy mounds that encircled the village. (The Sleepers, they were called, no one knew why.) Icy, frosty dusk was really thickening now; the mounds had turned dove gray and did look much like great curled-up sleeping beasts.

"Don't let him find me," Joe whispered to them as he ran dodging among them; by and by he was fairly certain that he had shaken off the stranger's pursuit, but in order to make even more certain he took the road to Chew Malreward and walked along it for a couple of miles, then circled back by a bridlepath. The moon climbed up, and then slid behind a bank of black cloud; but before it did so, a wink of something bright in the hedge bank caught Joe's eye: bright, a small circle of light, it was, and he put his hand into a tussock and pulled out a wineglass, with a round bowl and a stem the length of his two middle fingers placed end to end.

"Well, there's a queer thing!" muttered Joe. "Who could have been drinking wine out here in the middle of no-man's-land? And left his glass behind? Folk on a picnic last summer? Reckon I'll never know."

The glass was neither chipped nor cracked nor broken; when he had cleaned out a few sodden leaves with a swatch of grass, it gleamed sharp as crystal. Mrs. Honeysett would be pleased to have it, Joe thought, and checked a stab of pain, remembering the row of dusty tumblers unused on the shelf in his own home, locked now and shuttered.

Still, coming on the glass like that had someway lightened his spirits; he felt hope rise in him as he trudged along, clasping the stem of the glass, holding it in front of him as if it were a flagstaff. Hope of what? He hardly knew.

When the rain began, first a few drops, then a drenching downpour, he held the glass even more carefully upright, for a question had slid into his mind: would there be enough rain, before he reached the village, to fill the glass right up to its brim? Perhaps there might, he thought; just perhaps. Heaven knows *he* was wet right through his duffel jacket to his skin, and his boots scrunched with water as he walked. One good thing, in such weather as this, most probably the stranger would have given up his prying and his prowling, and would be shut away snug in the bar parlor of The Rose Revived.

By the time that Joe made his way over the hump-backed bridge, the glass was brim full. Not another drop of rain would it hold. Maybe it doesn't matter about the stranger after all, Joe thought joyfully; and so he went straight to the school, let himself in by the little back door, which was never locked, and watered the rose.

At ten minutes to midnight Lord Roderick Jeffreys's limousine softly re-entered Wish Wintergreen; it glided over the hump-backed bridge and came to a stop in the shadows by the church. The night was wild now; huge gusts of wind roared and rollicked; as the chauffeur got out and stepped to open the car door for his master, a massive stone griffin dislodged itself from the cornice of the church and came crashing down onto the car roof, trapping the man inside, who yelled with agony.

"Saunders, Saunders! Get me out of here! I think my leg's broken! Get me out!"

"I can't, sir," gasped the driver, wrestling with the smashed door lock.

"Well then phone the police! Phone for an ambulance! Ring somebody's doorbell. Bang on their doors!"

The chauffeur rang and knocked at house after house, but nobody seemed to hear his calls and tattoos. Either the inhabitants of Wish Wintergreen were a set of uncommonly sound sleepers—or else none of them was at home. Not even at the jail could Saunders raise any response. And the phone-box on the green was, as usual, out of order.

Doggedly, finding nothing better to do, the chauffeur began walking along the road to Mendip Magna.

And the wind began to drop.

In the village school, all was dark and silent. Not a shoe squeaked, not a corset creaked, not a bracelet clinked. Yet the whole population of the village was there, packed in tight and soundless, like mice in a burrow, intently watching: children breathless, kneeling, squatting and crouching in front, while their parents stood in a circle behind them. Fred Nightingale was there, and Joseph Mathinwell, his hands resting on the shoulders of his son Joe in front of him. All their eyes were fixed on one thing, the rose that was slowly growing out of a crack between two floorboards in the center of the room.

It was a white rose; that they all remembered afterward. But that was the only point on which their recollections did agree. About all else, their memories were at variance. Size? Big enough to fill the whole room. Or tiny, no larger than a clenched fist; but every single petal clear and distinctly visible, though you could see clean through, like a print on a photographic negative. The flower cast a shadow of light, as other objects cast a shadow of darkness. Scent? The whole school was imbued with its shadow and its fragrance. Fragrance of what? Apples, cucumber, lilac, violets? No, none of those things. Like nothing in the world, but never to be forgotten. The leaves, in their tracery of delicate outline, of an equal beauty with the flower.

Now, as the flower itself opened wider and wider, the

watchers found that their hearts almost stopped beating from terror. Terror? Why? Because how much longer could it continue to grow and expand its petals? How many more seconds had they left to marvel at this wonder? They clasped each other's hands, they held their breath. For all in the room five seconds, ten seconds, seemed to lengthen into a millennium of time. Then the church clock struck the first note of midnight, and, as it did so, swifter than a patch of sunlight leaving a cornfield, the rose was gone. Nothing remained but a faint fragrance.

Nobody spoke. *Think* they might, but their thoughts were locked inside them. Quiet as leaves, the villagers dispersed, each to his own home, children stumbling dreamily, clasping the hands of parents, lovers arm in arm, old and young, friends, grandchildren and grandparents lost in recollection.

Only Joseph Mathinwell paused a moment by the jail door to exchange a few quiet words with the stranger, who had been there too, at the back of the group, as was proper for an outsider.

"You'll be taking it back then—the root, and the trowel? And the basket of earth? To where it came from?" Joseph sighed.

"Yes," the stranger answered him. "It should never have been brought away. For thousands of years I and my fathers before me have searched. The duty was laid on us. Now the search is over; restitution will be made.

The gap will be filled. Farewell then, my friend, Joseph Mathinwell."

"Farewell, Duke Michael."

The prisoner turned and walked back into the jail; Fred Nightingale locked him in.

The trial of Joseph Mathinwell had to be adjourned because of the injuries to Judge Jeffreys, who had two broken legs. But before a new judge was summoned, the prisoner had agreed to reveal where he had found the wooden trowel. It had been under the floor of the village school, he said. When officials from the London museum visited the school, however, it became plain that someone had been there before them. Four square feet of earth, approximately, had been removed from beneath the floorboards. Mathinwell obviously could not have done it, for he had been in jail; nobody else in the village could throw any light on the matter. The prisoner was duly released, and went about his business. The school smelt faintly of roses, and does to this day.

The inhabitants of Wish Wintergreen, never a chatty lot at any time, walk about even quieter these days, with a solemn, happy, inward, recollected look about them. Sometimes, at night, they may glance up at the planet Saturn, in a friendly recognizing way, as if they looked over the hedge at the garden next door. They do not speak about these things. They are used to keeping secrets. But if anything at all hopeful is to happen in the world, there may be a good chance that it will have its beginnings in the village of Wish Wintergreen.

> In that garden, the raven utters no cry,
> The lion kills not.
> In that garden, the wolf snatches not the lamb,
> The sick man says not 'I am sick' . . .

The Happiest Sheep
in London

I'm going to explain how it all began, what caused such a disgraceful state of affairs.

The reason why John Sculpin and his mother moved up to London was because John had been offered a very good job. At least his mother thought it a very good job; John wasn't so sure whether any job was good. He had just left school and wanted to look around.

They had found a little house in Rumbury Town. Rumbury Town is a rather wild part of London, but the house was all right; it had a mimosa tree in the back yard and a round blue sign above the front door that said, "Marcus Magus, Alchymyste, dweltte in ysse Howse inne Fyfteene Sixtye."

The house was very old and cornery and cupboardy.

John's job was this: he was paid twelve pounds a week by the Drawing Board to erase Objectionable Inscriptions and Drawings from the walls of tube stations. He had a bicycle and a bucket and two bits of foam rubber, one wet, one dry. Whenever somebody rang up and said they had seen an Objectionable Inscription, John would fill his bucket with water and get on his bike and go along to the spot and scrub it off.

Of course, people don't always agree about what is objectionable. Sometimes, when John got there and found RUMBRY HIGH IS A HORABIL SKOOL, or *Down with Leeds United,* or *This Station is filthy,* or *i hate Delia Buggins,* he felt that people were making a fuss about nothing. Sometimes he felt like leaving the inscription where it was. But as he had often ridden a long way with his bucket and sponges, he nearly always rubbed the words off.

On the whole, he quite liked the job. At least he had plenty of chances to look around London. There was just one awkward thing: nearly all the Objectionable Inscriptions seemed to get written up at night. So John soon fell into the habit of staying awake at night and doing his sleeping by day.

In a way, that was how the trouble started.

One day about tea time, John's mother came home from shopping in Rumbury Market. She loved the market because everything was so cheap there. She had bought a coal scuttle, and a fan, and a pair of skating boots, and a lamp, and some golf clubs, and a collapsible wheelchair. The wheelchair was the only thing she actually needed; she bought the rest because they were being sold at bargain prices. The wheelchair was for their sheep, Melba. Mrs. Sculpin liked to take Melba for a walk in the park every day, but the park was a long way from their house and Melba was a slow walker; the chair would be a decided help in getting Melba quickly through the streets of Rumbury Town where people were not used to sheep anyway.

Well, Mrs. Sculpin came home, put down all her purchases on the step, found her key, and opened the door.

The inside of the house was a bit of a shock to her.

It had gone all rainbow-colored.

"My gracious stars!" said Mrs. Sculpin.

She sat down abruptly in Melba's chair, which rolled backward until it met the grandfather clock. Mrs. Sculpin got out of it and began wandering about. The rainbow colors seemed to have leaked, in a gooey way, out from under the door of the stair cupboard. As she watched, they spread farther and farther, up the walls and ceilings, over every bit of the house. When she opened the cupboard itself, she found a whole lot more rainbow, rolled up like a mattress.

"Well here's a fine old set to," Mrs. Sculpin said. She opened her mouth wide and shouted, "John! Jooooohn!"

It was just about time he got up, anyway.

John came downstairs in his pajamas, yawning.

"What's up, Ma?" he said.

Now during the daytime, if his mother was out, John sometimes answered the door when people came delivering things—coal and laundry and the kind of letters you have to sign for. He had learned how to do this in his sleep without really waking. So now his mother said,

"John, *John*, what*ever* have you let somebody leave at our house?"

John rubbed his eyes a bit and looked around.

"Why, anyone can see what it is, Ma, it's a rainbow."

"I never ordered a rainbow," said Mrs. Sculpin. "What would I want a *rainbow* for, tell me that?"

"*I* dunno," said John. Then he yawned a bit more and said, "But nobody left it, Ma. At least, I didn't open the door to anybody."

"How did it get here, then?"

"Maybe it just came. Has it been raining?" John said. He went out the back door and felt the yellow mimosa blossoms in the yard. They were all damp and fluffy.

"John! Come in out of the yard at once in your pajamas!"

"Been raining, all right," said John, coming back.

"Why should the rainbow end in *our* stair cupboard?"

"Got to end somewhere, hasn't it?"

"Well I'm not having it here," said Mrs. Sculpin. She tried sweeping, she tried dusting, she tried vacuuming. But she couldn't shift the rainbow.

"It's so *upsetting*," she grumbled to Mrs. Jones next door.

John rather liked it. The colors kept moving around. One minute the stairs would be pink, the next they were lime green. The kitchen might flow from orange to indigo and back to primrose.

Another person who enjoyed the change was Melba.

She was a homely sheep ("Plain, downright plain," her mother had said at first sight of her, "our Melba's never going to win any beauty contests, that's for sure.") Melba was not vain, she didn't worry about her looks, but she did enjoy sitting down in a bright purple or jade green patch of light and then studying her appearance in the glass. Of course it would have been even nicer to keep the colors on when she rode in her wheelchair through the streets of Rumbury Town, but you can't have everything.

Another member of the family who, like Mrs. Sculpin, disapproved of the rainbow, was the cat, Euston. Euston was quite young (they had got him as a kitten from Euston Station Left Luggage Department where someone had left him in a paper bag and never returned to claim him) but although he was young he was very dignified. His own color was a pale putty, like powdered ginger, with amber eyes, and he did not at all relish suddenly being turned rose red or royal blue. Besides, he found that all these fancy colors discouraged the mice, who did not care to venture out of their holes into such a blaze of red and blue and green.

Mrs. Sculpin rang up the local Council.

"I want you to come and take away a lot of rainbow that's got into my house," she said.

"That'll call for a Special Rubbish Disposal Unit," said the man at the other end. "There will be a charge of two pounds."

"*Two pounds!*" cried Mrs. Sculpin. "I'm not paying

two pounds to have a rainbow removed. A rainbow's an Act of Nature, you ought to take it away free."

"If it's an Act of Nature, you'd better try the Natural History Museum," suggested the Council Officer.

So she tried the Natural History Museum. They sent around a professor with a light meter and a hydrograph and a barometer and a rainbow meter, but all he did was to take measurements and samples; then he went off on his tricycle saying that he would let them know.

"When?" Mrs. Sculpin called after him sharply.

"Oh, it shouldn't take more than a year. . . ."

"I'm not waiting a year," said Mrs. Sculpin, and she rang the Natural Gas Board.

But they said they only dealt in Natural Gas, not Natural Light.

So then she rang the Light and Power Board, but they said they only dealt in plain light, not colored.

Then she rang the people who come and suck out drains when they get blocked; the Highways, Sewers and Public Cleansing Department. This lot was more obliging. They sent a great tanker-truck with a long suction pipe, stuck the end of the pipe through Mrs. Sculpin's front door, and sucked and sucked. But all they sucked in was Euston, which did not at all improve his disposition. He had to be rescued from inside the tanker, and Mrs. Sculpin had to wash him in Kittyclens. The rainbow stayed where it was, all over the house.

A great many neighbors wandered along to watch while the sucking went on.

"*Whatever* can Mrs. Sculpin have *in* there?" they asked each other.

A man from the *Rumbury Borough News* heard that something peculiar was afoot; he came and looked through the Sculpins' front door, then hurried back to his office and wrote a piece for his paper about the Rumbury Town rainbow.

Next day all the national newspapers printed the story too.

WIDOW FIGHTS LOCAL GOVERNMENT OFFICIALS OVER UNWANTED RAINBOW, they said.

Mrs. Sculpin tried the Citizens' Advice Bureau, as well as *Which, Where, What*, and *Why*. Nobody could help her. A paint firm came and painted her house, free, but the rainbow stayed on top of the paint. A beetle-killing firm blew thick white fumes through the house. Euston caught a cold, but the rainbow didn't budge.

Meanwhile a gang of international gold thieves read about the case in the *Continental Daily Mail*. This gang were known as the Hatmen, because they all wore such large hats that very little of them could be seen above the knees. No one had ever seen their faces.

"We must fly to England at once," said the leader of the gang, Filippo Fedora.

So they caught the next plane and flew to London from Paris, where they had their headquarters, arousing a lot of interest on the journey, because they smoked their cigars and ate their airline snacks through holes in their hats.

They took rooms at the Rumbury Temperance Hotel and settled down to watch the movements of the Sculpin family.

It was easy for them to keep watch unobserved, lolling against lamp posts, leaning against street corners, concealed by their hats. People are used to odd characters in Rumbury Town; nobody took any notice of them.

Mrs. Sculpin was still trying to get rid of her rainbow.

She called the Borough Surveyor, who came and surveyed it. After he had surveyed it for a long time, he said,

"My heart leaps up when I survey
A rainbow in the cupboard;
But how to siphon it away
Has not yet been discovered."

And he climbed into his Mini and drove back to the Surveying Department.

"The movements of that family are very, very simple," said Filippo Fedora to his second-in-command, Sandro Sombrero. "The son goes out at night. The mother goes out in the daytime. All we have to do is lure *her* out at night too, and the house will be empty."

"What about the cat, and that sheep?"

"We shall have to lure them out as well. Start thinking how to do it."

The whole gang thought hard, sitting under their hats in Rumbury Fields.

The next day Mrs. Sculpin had a telephone call. Her hands were all soapy when she answered the phone; she had been mixing up a massive brew of bleach, soap powder, detergent, washing soda, and Polygone dye remover in her automatic washing machine.

"Hullo, who is it?"

"Is that Mrs. Sculpin? *Daisy* Sculpin? Daisy! It's great to hear your voice! This is your cousin Etta, from Sunrise, Alaska. Etta Biretta! I'm in London, Daisy!"

"I didn't know I had a cousin Etta, let alone in Sunrise, Alaska."

"Oh, yes, Daisy, your great-uncle Fred Sculpin married twice, and his second wife's third son was my grandfather's aunt's second cousin once removed, Bernard Biretta, my cousin Bernie, so *I'm* your fourth cousin twice removed."

"Fancy," said Mrs. Sculpin, who hadn't quite followed. "How long are you in London for, Etta? We're a bit at sixes and sevens, here, but maybe you'd care to come in for a cup of tea, say, Tuesday fortnight?"

"No, no, no, Daisy dear, you must come out with *me*, this very night, because I am flying back to Sunrise at nine tomorrow morning. So hop in a cab right away, and come along down, and mind you bring dear little John, I'm just longing to meet him, and of course darling Melba and Euston too, it'll be just wonderful to see you all."

"How do you know so much about us if I never heard of *you?*" asked Mrs. Sculpin, rather puzzled.

"Why, I read about you in the papers, you're famous people, dearie! I can't wait to meet you. So hop in that cab and come along down."

"Well," said Mrs. Sculpin, "all right. I'm afraid John won't be able to come, because of his job, but I'll bring the others. You'll have to wait just a little, because I was putting in some washing, but I'll start as soon as I can."

"Do that, Daisy!"

"Here, though," said Mrs. Sculpin, "where do I have to come *to*?"

"The Old Alaska Fried Chicken Parlor in Piccadilly."

"All right," said Mrs. Sculpin, and she put down the receiver.

"I'm going out to dinner, John," she said.

"Coo, Ma, who with?"

"Cousin Etta Biretta from Sunrise, Alaska. Your supper's in the oven, and I've just started the washing machine. If it hasn't switched itself off by ten, will *you* switch it off, please? It's been making a kind of gloop-gloop noise lately, and I don't trust it."

Mrs. Sculpin had bought the washing machine secondhand in Rumbury Market. It cost only two pounds twenty, which seemed almost too cheap for such a very large machine.

Mrs. Sculpin strapped Melba into the wheelchair, squeezed Euston into a shopping basket which she carried over her arm, and set off. She did not take a cab, as that would be extravagant, and she was a thrifty woman. She knew the way to Piccadilly and it was only an hour's walk. She might take a cab home, if it was raining, or late.

Cousin Etta became quite impatient, waiting at the

Fried Chicken Parlor. She began to wonder if something had gone wrong.

Mrs. Sculpin trudged through Canning Town and Kentish Town and Camden Town and along the Euston Road.

Meanwhile her son John had a telephone call.

"Is that Mr. John Sculpin?" The caller had a slight foreign accent. "There is an Objectionable Inscription at Cockfosters Tube Station."

"What does it say?" John had been about to take his supper out of the oven. He was not very keen to go out.

"It says, 'John Sculpin is a Silly Nit.' "

"Oh, very well," said John. "I'll come and remove it."

He found his pail and his two pieces of foam rubber, and wheeled out his bicycle. He forgot about switching off the washing machine; anyway, it was not yet ten. He left the oven on, so as to keep his supper warm. He locked the front door carefully and set out for Cockfosters, which is a long way up the Piccadilly Underground line, way out in the suburbs.

Two minutes after he had cycled off, five dark figures nipped over the garden wall, broke the kitchen window at the back of the house, under the mimosa tree, and climbed in.

The Sculpin house was pitch dark inside, and it was full of a tremendous rumbling sound, and a smell of overcooked supper.

"*Dio mio*, what's that?" said Carlo Capote.

"It is nothing, nothing at all. Merely the English central heating. Begin the search, there is no time to lose!"

After an hour's search, Diego Domino said,

"This smell of burning makes me nervous."

"Do not regard it! The English all prefer their food burned black. Continue the search!"

"We can't seem to find it anywhere, boss."

"Take up the floorboards, then!"

When Mrs. Sculpin finally arrived at the Old Alaska Fried Chicken Parlor, Cousin Etta rushed into the street to welcome her.

"Cousin Daisy, what kept you? Where have you *been*? Well, never mind, you're here at last, but I was so worried! Now this must be Melba, and this is Euston?" (She got them the wrong way round as she patted their heads, but neither of them noticed; Euston was eagerly breathing in the scent of Old Alaska Fried Chicken and Melba was wistfully looking at the beautiful signs in rainbow-colored lights above Piccadilly Circus and wishing that once— just once—she could sit up there among those lights and look at herself in a mirror.)

"My, it's just grand to see you all!" said Cousin Etta. "Now come in, come along in."

So they all went into the Fried Chicken Parlor.

Unfortunately by now it was quite late. In fact it was nearly closing time.

The owner gave a very unwelcoming look at Mrs. Sculpin and Euston and Melba.

He said, "I'm sorry, but it's closing time, and cats are

not allowed in this fried chicken parlor and sheep are *definitely* not allowed. I can't serve you. I must ask you to leave."

Everyone's faces fell at this. They had worked up quite brisk appetites on the long walk from Rumbury Town. Even Melba, though she did not fancy fried chicken, had noticed a huge panful of coleslaw behind the counter, and she was sniffing at it hungrily.

"*Not serve us?*" cried the horrified Cousin Etta. "Why, I've come all the way from Sunrise, Alaska, to see my cousin Daisy here, and besides, she's famous—she is the lady who has a rainbow in her stair cupboard."

"I don't care about that," said the owner. "I don't care if she has a monsoon in her pantry and a thunderstorm in her bathroom. I'm closing up."

"Wait a minute," said Mrs. Sculpin, who was always practical. "It says TAKE OUT FOOD on your sign. You don't want to leave all that fried chicken and salad lying here overnight, so why don't we take it away?"

Well, the owner didn't have any objection to that, he was pleased to get rid of it as sales had been poor that evening, so he picked up a whole crate of fried chicken, and shoveled all the coleslaw salad into a tub, and gave them a big bagful of Old Southern Style Cornpone Fritters, and another of Hushpuppies, and a jar of Pa's Persimmon Jelly, and a carton of Granma's Guzzly Gravy, and a pot of Goober Peas, and a plastic box packed tight with waffles and Snowshoe Syrup.

Melba stopped looking wistful as Mrs. Sculpin bal-

anced the tub of coleslaw on her wheelchair and put all
the other things on top.

"I'll be out finding a taxi while you pay, Etta dear,"
she said happily. "And then we can all go back to our
house in Rumbury Town. It will be much nicer having
dinner at home."

"Hey—wait a minute—"

Cousin Etta tried to grab Mrs. Sculpin at the door,
but the owner of the parlor thought she was trying to
leave without paying, and he soon put a stop to that. So
by the time Etta hurried out, Mrs. Sculpin had already
found an empty taxi. She didn't even hail one; it pulled
up beside her, and when it did she recognized the driver
as her next-door neighbor Mr. Jones. He, of course, had
no trouble in recognizing *her*, for you do not often see
ladies pushing sheep in wheelchairs around Piccadilly
Circus.

"Fancy meeting you here, Mrs. Sculpin. On your way
home, were you? I was just thinking of packing it in; I'll
be glad to take you back to Rumbury Town."

"Oh, thank you ever so, Mr. Jones! If you wouldn't
mind giving Melba a bit of a push—and helping me with
the wheelchair—that's right, Euston, you pop in and
mind the chicken—and this is my cousin Etta Biretta
from Sunrise, Alaska."

"Pleased to meet you," said Mr. Jones, and two minutes later he was whizzing them back to Rumbury Town
by all sorts of clever shortcuts so that it took no time to
get home. As they drove along Etta was racking her brains

to think of some other place than the Rumbury Temperance Hotel where they could eat their meal. She knew that Filippo Fedora would not be at all pleased to see them, either there or at the Sculpin house.

"You don't want to be bothered with me at your house, Daisy, so late in the evening—why don't we all go and have a picnic on Rumbury Marshes, I'm sure Melba would enjoy that—"

"But it's pitch dark and pouring with rain," said Mrs. Sculpin, which it was. "We can picnic just as well in my kitchen, Etta, there's lots of paper plates under the chicken. Besides, I'm a bit anxious about my washing machine. It's been going gloop-gloop lately."

Meanwhile John, on his bike, with his bucket and sponge, had cycled all the way through the rain to Cockfosters Station, and asked the station-master where he could find the Objectionable Inscription that said "John Sculpin is a Silly Nit."

The station-master was perplexed. He had no record of any such inscription. But he helped John search all over the station, from end to end; they did not find anything except a picture of a pig labeled "Frank," and an inscription that said I VOTED TORY AND I'M SORRY. John rubbed these off, and then he cycled all the way home again.

Back in Rumbury Town, a lot of things had been happening.

When Mr. Jones brought his taxi to a halt outside the Sculpin house, Cousin Etta gave a slight scream.

"What's the matter, Etta dear?"

"It's j-j-j-just that I'm not very used to t-t-traveling in t-t-taxis with sh-sheep!"

The real reason for Etta's scream was that she had noticed a policeman standing outside the Sculpin house and gazing thoughtfully at it.

He was staring at the house because, as he walked toward it, he had noticed lumps of foam floating from the upstairs windows.

"That's unusual," he thought. And he wondered whether maybe he ought to report the matter to the police station. While he stood there, scratching his head, he began to hear strange noises coming from the house.

And just as Mrs. Sculpin, Euston, Melba, and Cousin Etta climbed from Mr. Jones's taxi, and while John, tired and hungry, pedaled up on his bicycle, something exploded inside the house with a tremendous bang.

More foam shot out of the windows. Many of them broke. And some flames came from the downstairs windows as well.

The policeman decided that he had better call the station on his walkie-talkie. He called the Fire Brigade too.

"Oh, mercy," said Mrs. Sculpin. "That'll be the washing machine. I knew it would do that, one of these days."

"Nasty dangerous things," said the policeman. "Well, the Force is on its way, so is the Fire Brigade."

Cousin Etta didn't care for the sound of this.

"Oh, wow!" she cried, shading her eyes and staring

down the street. "Do my eyes deceive me, or isn't that my long-lost nephew, Benno Biretta? Benno, Benno, yoohoo, look who's here, it's your auntie, it's Aunt Etta, all the way from Sunrise, Alaska, wait till I catch up with you, Benno, Uncle Frank will be wanting to hear *all* about you!" And she darted off like a missile, and was not seen again by any of the persons in this story.

"Well!" said Mrs. Sculpin. "Impulsive! When we hadn't even tasted the fried chicken! Though how we're ever going to get to eat it I'm sure I don't know—"

While she was speaking, Euston, curious to investigate the noises in the house, had nipped through his cat flap in the front door. And Melba who, though a slow walker, was a champion hurdler, had popped in through the broken window.

"Oh, oh, they'll be drowned or burned," wailed Mrs. Sculpin. "Oh, please, somebody, rescue them—"

"I'll go, Ma," said John, and he unlocked the front door with his latchkey. Just then the Police and Fire Brigade arrived, so a lot of police and firemen raced in after him.

It was quite difficult to push their way through the foam, which was deep, up to their chins, and thick, like apple charlotte. There were bits of washing machine all over the kitchen. The kitchen stove was black, twisted, and upside down.

"I reckon the washing machine exploded," said a fireman.

"And the cooker caught on fire," said a policeman.

"Oh, gosh," said John. "I went out leaving my supper in the oven."

"You was lucky," said a fireman. "The foam from the washer put the fire out. Not much for us to do here, but pump out the foam for you."

"Watch out for Euston and Melba before you do that," warned John.

He looked for them, and saw Euston, who did not care for the foam, up on the mantelpiece, and Melba, buried to her ears in bubbles, standing on the edge of a large hole in the kitchen floor and gazing down into it. Everybody looked down into the hole, and there, also buried in foam, they were surprised to see the tops of five hats.

"That's a remarkable circumstance," said the police sergeant. "There would appear to be five persons down there in that hole. We'd best haul them out before you start your pumping, Mr. Critchwell."

So the five people, who had been helplessly pinned down by the weight of foam on their hats, were hauled up, and the sergeant, always one to read the Interpol Circulars, at once recognized them as members of the notorious Hatmen gang, and had handcuffs put on them while they were still weak and sneezing from the bubbles.

"It is unfair!" hissed Filippo Fedora. "Is a trap you set for us! You think you are clever, huh, with your big bangs and your foam bombs and your phoney rainbows!"

"What were you doing in Mrs. Sculpin's cellar?"

"We look for the pot of gold, naturalmente," said Carlo

Capote, and earned a scowl from Filippo Fedora through the slit in his hat.

"Pot of gold?"

"Pot of gold at rainbow's end."

"Well, I do call that cheek!" said Mrs. Sculpin. "What was to stop you coming to the front door and ringing the bell, 'stead of knocking a hole in my kitchen floor? And why you had to ruin my vinyl tiles when there's perfectly good steps down from the stair cupboard to the cellar I do *not* know. And anyway, we gave the pot of gold to the gentleman from the Natural History Museum—ever such a long time ago—as I could have told you if you'd come and asked, civil."

"Oh," said Filippo.

So he and the rest of the Hatmen—Carlo Capote, Diego Domino, Sandro Sombrero, and Luigi Leghorn— were taken to the police station and charged with breaking and entering and being in possession of offensive weapons; to wit, daggers, hammers, chisels, and safebreakers' tools.

The rest of the party, once the foam was pumped out, sat down in Mrs. Sculpin's kitchen to eat fried chicken, coleslaw, Cornpone Fritters, Hushpuppies, Persimmon Jelly, Guzzly Gravy, Goober Peas, waffles, and Snowshoe Syrup. Euston had all the wishbones. Melba was given a huge bowl of coleslaw, but she had been washed so dazzlingly clean by all the foam that she kept forgetting to eat, as she studied her reflection in a large metal dish cover.

"Coo!" said John suddenly, in the middle of a bite of chicken. "The rainbow's gone!"

"So I should hope," said his mother, "seeing I stuffed the whole length of it into the washing machine with half a stone of soap powder, eight bottles of bleach, a laundry-size packet of detergent, a sack of soda, and a whole carton of Polygone dye remover."

"No wonder the washing machine exploded," said John.

"Dangerous things," said the chief fireman, swallowing his last bite of waffle and rising to take his leave.

"I'll look for another in Rumbury Market tomorrow," said Mrs. Sculpin.

But the next day they had a letter from the Natural History Museum to say that, since the pot of gold from their stair cupboard was undoubtedly *gold*, it counted as treasure trove, and therefore belonged to the Crown. On the other hand, since it had been decided by a body of learned judges that the pot of gold had not been hidden in the stair cupboard by any person or persons, but was *res naturae*, or an Act of Nature, it was *not* treasure trove, and therefore belonged to Mrs. Sculpin and John, who had found it. Taking these two decisions together, they had agreed that half the gold should go to the Crown, and the other half, worth forty-eight million pounds, check enclosed, to Mrs. Sculpin and John.

"Maybe you better get a *new* washing machine, Ma," said John, "not another of these bargain buys."

"What pleases *me* is that we're rid of the rainbow,"

said Mrs. Sculpin. "That's the best thing so far as *I'm* concerned."

But when she left the house to go to the electricity showrooms she found that the rainbow had not been dissolved or turned white by all her washing as she supposed. It had been blown by the explosion into the streets of Rumbury Town.

And there, in a thousand bits, splashed all over the Co-op and the tube station and the bank and the war memorial and the public baths, it still is.

Some people think it lowers the tone of the neighborhood; they have written to *The Times* complaining about it. Other people, John for instance, quite enjoy having a pink post office and a sky blue library and a peach-colored police station.

And Melba, the happiest sheep in London, sits bathed in brilliant colors from end to end of Rumbury High Street as her wheelchair glides along.

The Fire Dogs

Every day the two old ladies, Miss Wilhelmina Martingale and Miss Roberta Martingale, went out driving. They drove across the park that surrounded their house, Martingale Old Hall, and then right through the city of Thornwick, which now surrounded Martingale Park in every direction.

The old ladies did not approve of motorcars; they used a little electric brougham, dark green and claret colored, with big brass lamps and fittings, and solid rubber tires. It bowled along quite silently at fifteen miles an hour.

"So greatly preferable to those noisy, vulgar automobiles," said Miss Martingale, operating the handle that steered the neat vehicle. The handle moved backward or forward to start or stop, and sideways for direction.

Everybody in Thornwick city was well used to the sight of the old ladies on their daily outing, sitting bolt upright, side by side, in their high, bone-stiffened lace collars, with feather or fur boas draped around their shoulders, and hats like huge complicated pancakes piled very high with all kinds of fruit, flowers, and plumes. If it rained, one large claret-colored umbrella was mounted between the seats, which protected them both.

Most people gave the sisters an indulgent or admiring smile as they passed by; strangers tended to gape in amazement, sometimes laughed, sometimes asked if there was a picture of them on sale at newsstands.

But there was one person in the town who had looked at them with envy and hatred for many many years.

In order to reach real country the old ladies had to pass through some heavy city traffic. But the other cars, buses, and trucks always gave way to them very considerately, and never a scratch had marked the green shiny sides of the brougham in all its years of life; not even one of its brass fittings had ever been dented.

This was partly on account of the Fire Dogs who ran ahead.

Long, long ago, back in historical times when lordly households were large and labor was cheap, proud and wealthy noblemen sometimes used to employ running footmen, servants whose task it was to race along the highway at top speed, warning everybody on the road to get out of the way at once, for their master's carriage was close behind. But the ancient lords of Martingale (and the family went back earlier than Saxon times) never bothered with such a piece of cruel display.

What they had, instead, from Norman times on, were the Fire Dogs.

UP THE CHIMNEY DOWN

A crusading member of the family, Sir Gervas Martingale, had brought back a pair of hounds from the mountains west of Baalbek, and their descendants had been with the family ever since. Big, black, rangy dogs they were, with feathery fur, not long, nor short; low-slung tails, large feet, silky, dangling ears, intelligent topaz eyes, and long narrow laughing faces. It was said that the first Fire Dog and his mate had belonged to the High King Solomon, that they had run ahead of his carriage when he went to meet the Queen of Sheba; and certainly the hounds carried themselves very stately, like dogs of royal heritage and breeding. When they stood, they reached to the height of a table, and they were calm, quiet dogs, who seldom barked, never involved themselves in fights or hunting, or the other activities of commoner breeds. They merely kept themselves in readiness for their daily task; and when the lords of Martingale drove abroad, or rode across their land, the two Fire Dogs were always ahead of them, side by side, keeping up a regular steady pace that looked deceptively easy and smooth, but was as fast as the hard gallop of a horse, and could continue all day, as far as any horse could travel, without tiring. In their mouths they carried the flaming torches which had brought them their name.

These torches were set into right-angled bracket hold-ers, to prevent the flames from blowing back into the dogs' faces. The flames never went out, being fed by some Eastern mixture of oils and minerals, the secret of which

214

Sir Gervas had brought back with him from Baalbek along with the dogs.

Strangers to Thornwick were naturally startled to see the two big, graceful animals loping along, never losing nor gaining pace, wearing emerald-studded collars, carrying their flaming, smoking torches, which cast sparks behind them on the wind. Only once had anyone ever tried to stop them; and the tale of how badly he had been burned was enough to put anyone else off from making such an attempt.

On the whole, the natives of Thornwick city were proud of their old ladies. And there was more to the Fire Dogs than met the eye, some people said. They would lead you wherever you wanted to go. "Take me to El Dorado—or the Islands of the Hesperides—or Shangri-La—or Mysteriour Kor—or the Black City of Hidden Troy—or the Garden of Eden!" you could order the Fire Dogs, and they would obediently dash off, and if you followed them they would lead you to the place of your heart's desire, wherever it was, no matter how distant in time or space.

"So why don't the Martingale ladies ever get the dogs to take them anywhere like that?" a girl called Hetty Sark once demanded of her mother as the two of them plodded homeward through the wet and slush, carrying heavy bundles of laundry, while the Fire Dogs raced past them on the highway, ahead of the little green-and-wine-colored chariot with its gleaming brass fittings, and the two sisters snugly wrapped in sable and velvet.

"Why? Because they are two toffee-nosed old stick-in-the-muds, that's why!" coughed Hetty's mother, and then paused to spit angrily in the gutter. "They think their own way is too good to leave it for any other. Don't you be like that, Hetty, girl! When you grow up, you look about you, and choose the best, and put out your hand and take it!"

Sometimes foreigners—businessmen, perhaps, from Liverpool or Birmingham or Paris—complained to the traffic police if one of their limousines had been stuck for ten minutes while the elderly Martingale sisters negotiated Pigiron Crossing, or Worsted Junction, where six highways met, but complaints got little sympathy from the police.

"Let the old girls have their outing, what does it matter if the traffic does get held up a bit? The Martingale family has done plenty of good to the town," said the Chief of Police.

True enough, in Thornwick there was a Martingale Free Hospital, a Martingale Free Library, a Martingale Theater, swimming pool, amusement park, old people's home, art gallery, billiard hall, technical college, girls' school, and Electric Palace, all due to the generosity of the family.

"Besides," people said, "old Miss Wilhelmina and Miss Roberta are the last of the family; there won't be any more Martingales when they are gone. Let them ride while they can."

It was so. The sisters were the last of the Martingales, though they themselves did not seem particularly sad about it.

"Families have to age and die, just like the trees in the park," said Miss Wilhelmina to Miss Roberta, as they drove across Thornwick Royal Circus, inconveniencing no end of trams, trolley buses, trucks, buses, and faster moving taxis and cars as they carefully negotiated the wide sweep and complicated junction. "So why should ours be any exception?"

"I don't mind going," replied Miss Roberta as the brougham proceeded on its way, chugging doggedly up the steep climb toward Thornwick High Moor and open country. "And it is an excellent plan that Martingale Hall should be turned into a convalescent home after our death. But I confess I do worry a little about Sigma and Tau. How will they fare, supposing that they outlive us?"

Sigma and Tau were the two Fire Dogs. Like the sisters, they were the last of their line. Each previous generation of Fire Dogs had always produced two offspring, just two, to maintain the succession; but Sigma, as if understanding that there would be no more need, had never given birth to puppies.

"I am quite sure that Jamieson will find them a good home, with people of discrimination," said Miss Wilhelmina. Jamieson was the bailiff of the Martingale estate.

I am not sure that I entirely trust Jamieson, thought Miss Roberta. Sometimes I think that I see a calculating look in his eye. Aloud, she said, "I should not like to think of them going to a zoo. There they would have no proper purpose in living. Idleness would not suit them."

Arrived at the top of Thornwick High Moor—from which seventeen counties could be seen—the sisters would sit for a while, enjoying the view, under parasols in the summer, wrapped in thick plaid rugs if it was winter, beside the huge, steeple-shaped rock that was called Garm's Crag. Before sipping a little brandy from a flask, the ladies would give a bowl of broth to the Fire Dogs, who would be at the rock already when they arrived, waiting in dignity, their torches put aside into iron rings that some earlier Martingale ancestor had set into the rock for the purpose.

Then, after everybody had rested, Miss Wilhelmina would nod to the dogs, who would take up their torches again and trot off ahead, while the sisters returned to the city, this time with Miss Roberta at the control handle.

All along the route, the people of the town bowed, or waved, or smiled, or tipped caps as they passed by, and the sisters bowed graciously in acknowledgment.

The Fire Dogs, of course, did not acknowledge people's waves or smiles. They kept up their steady pace, concentrated on their duty, and looked only straight ahead. But all the time they ran in front of the electric carriage, connecting thoughts flew back and forth between the two of them, spinning an invisible web.

Don't you wish that sometimes our mistresses would choose a different road? Day after day we run the same way, when there is a whole world to choose from! Oh, the sorrow of the smells and sounds that we never scent or hear, the sights that we never see! My heart aches for the roads that we never tread, the forests we never enter, the rivers that we never swim.

Hush! We have our task to perform as our parents did before us, and theirs before them, back as far as the High King himself. We are not common hounds, we are the Fire Dogs. Because we pace our narrow way with such devotion, we have a strength in us greater than other creatures.

What good is this strength in us, if it is never put to use?

Hush! Wait! The time is not yet come!

In the city of Thornwick there was one person who neither smiled nor waved at sight of the Martingale sisters. This was the person known as Mrs. Muesli.

Children had given her this name behind her back because she mumbled her jaws all the time like a person who is eating cereal with nuts in it. She was a sharp-featured middle-aged woman with her hair done up in a big iron-gray knob. She lived in a big red-brick house just outside the gates of Martingale Park; every day she looked out through her front window to see the sisters drive past. Twice she would look out, as they drove out and as they returned, and each time she saw them she shook her fist at them.

"Let them just wait!" she muttered. "Let them just wait a little longer!"

This was the history of Mrs. Muesli: As a girl, Hetty Sark, she had lived in the slums at the poor end of Thornwick. Her father had died of drink; her mother took in washing for a living. The life of Hetty and her mother was hard, poor, and wretched. Sometimes Hetty, watching the Fire Dogs dash past, ahead of Miss Wilhelmina and Miss Roberta, who, in those days, were young and beautiful—sometimes Hetty would think, "It's unfair! Why should they have all that, and I have nothing?" And she made a vow: "One day, by hook or by crook, *I* shall have those Fire Dogs!"

After her mother had died, Hetty went to earn her living as a scullery maid. Then she became a kitchen maid. Then she rose to become a lady's maid. Then, with good recommendations, she went to work for the Duchess of Wessex, as her personal maid, at a high wage. Ten years went by. The Duchess boasted to all her friends that she had the best lady's maid in the country.

One of Hetty's tasks, before any important party, was to fetch the Dutchess's strongbox of jewels from the bank where they were kept. This would happen two or three times a month. Each time Hetty went to the bank, she presented a note from the Duchess, authorizing Miss Hetty Sark to collect the jewels. But on one occasion the guard at the bank laid down the note on a table instead of putting it in a drawer. Quick as a flash, when his head was turned the other way, Hetty slipped the piece of paper back into her pocket.

The note was dated May 3, and the year.

Twenty-eight days later, Hetty returned to the bank. She had written in a figure 1 after the 3, very, very carefully, in the same ink that the Duchess of Wessex always used. The guard at the bank recognized Hetty, recognized the note and the writing, saw that it was dated May 31, which was that day's date, went and fetched the strongbox, and gave it to Hetty. Quiet and demure, she walked out of the bank, carrying the heavy box in her arms.

But there was no Rolls Royce waiting outside.

The Duchess never saw her jewels nor her maid again.

What did Hetty do?

She put herself through school: history, mathematics, geography, physics, and the rest. She took her O-levels, one of them in Witchcraft. Then she did A-levels, one in Advanced Witchcraft.

Then she went away to Esclairmonde College, where Differential Sorcery, Extended Witchcraft, Higher Necromancy, Ephesian Letters, Divining, Pure and Applied Voodoo, electrobiology, and Revised Runes were on the syllabus. Hetty studied all these subjects; she was a slow, dogged, but successful student. It was a thirteen-year course, and cost all her savings from the Duchess's stolen diamond tiaras and carcanets. But when she left the college, Hetty was able, of course, to earn her living in a dozen different ways: by casting runes, predicting international events, altering the weather, helping people who were suffering from the Evil Eye, or laying on a bit of Evil Eye herself.

She did these things to pay the rent. But she was not interested in them. What she wanted was the Fire Dogs.

"They can take you anywhere you want to go," Hetty's mother had told her, as she lay gasping and dying in the Martingale Infirmary. "Those Fire Dogs could lead you on to the planet Saturn if you wanted to go there."

Hetty wasn't sure if she wanted to go to the planet Saturn, but she thought about it carefully. During the ten years spent working in other people's back kitchens and dining rooms, the ten years with the Duchess of Wessex, and the thirteen years at Esclairmonde College, Hetty's ideas about where she wanted to be taken went through various changes. When she was young, cold, and hungry, she thought she would ask the dogs to take her somewhere warm and cheerful; Babylon, perhaps, or the Elysian Fields, Arcadia, maybe, or Miami Beach. Then, after a few years at college, where she was not at all popular with her fellow students, her tastes had changed, and she thought she would prefer to be taken somewhere interesting, mysterious, and classy: Cephalonia, the lost island; or Valhalla; or Dilmun; or Xanadu.

Now her tastes had changed again.

Day by day she sat at her window, spinning a rope made out of cobwebs and her own thin gray hair; it looked as fine as threads of mohair wool, but was stronger than steel cable.

Spinning it took another two years; human hair grows slowly, and spiders will not spin their webs to order.

During those two years, Hetty had plenty of time to

think where she would like to go. Sometimes she made a little extra money from divination or thaumaturgy or dowsing or clairvoyance; enough to pay for travel books as well as her rent, and the bread and butter and tea which was all she ate.

At the end of two years the cobweb rope was finished.

Then, one day, as the electric brougham came sliding past, Hetty flung her rope across the road. The cobweb immediately tightened, as if invisible hands on the other side had caught it, and the two elderly sisters were flung violently backward out of their seats onto the hard ground. Both of them were killed instantly.

A week later, two great trees grew up, one on either side of the road: a silver birch and a copper beech.

And the following week Martingale Old Hall was turned into a convalescent hospital. All the old ladies' belongings, their clothes, furniture, bottles of lavender water, books, safety pins, and handkerchiefs, were put up for sale by auction. The Fire Dogs were for sale too. Mrs. Muesli had bribed Jamieson the bailiff to put the dogs into the sale instead of giving them to the Queen as he had been instructed.

Hundreds of people came to the sale. Mrs. Muesli was there too. She knew, of course, that she must obtain the Fire Dogs by fair purchase if they were to be of any use to her.

The dogs came quite far down on the sale list, and when the time was coming toward their turn, more and more people pushed into the Auction Rooms. The Fire

Dogs sat in dignity on the platform, one on each side of the auctioneer, and people began to bid for them. There was Miss Margie Prebble, the TV animal expert, who was after them and prepared to bid up to ten thousand; so was the owner of a circus; Sir Marcus Drippie, a scientist, wanted them for experimental purposes and had a huge grant from a chemical firm; then there was Lord Hagridden, who wanted to buy them for breeding. And there were plenty of other would-be purchasers, all equally keen.

But strangely enough, almost at once, all these people began to drop out of the bidding. Miss Margie Prebble was afflicted by a sudden violent headache, and had to run out for some hot tea and aspirin. The circus owner sprained his tonsils, shouting, and had to be taken to the first aid room and then to the hospital. Tom Vonderbilt, who wanted to make a film about the Fire Dogs, sprained his back standing up to make a bid and had to sit down again in frightful agony. Sir Marcus Drippie was called out to take an important telephone call. Lord Hagridden was suddenly overcome by paralysis, and could neither speak nor move for two hours.

And the lady known as Mrs. Muesli was able to buy Lot One Hundred and Two, a green and wine-colored electric carriage with two Fire Dogs, at a very reasonable price.

After the sale Mrs. Muesli went to inspect the dogs, who had been taken back to their enclosure, and they stared back at her calmly, neither barking, growling, nor wagging their plumy tails.

Mrs. Muesli surveyed them from head to toe with an exultant eye.

"You are mine now; do you understand?" she said to them. "From now on you have to do what I say. I have bought you with hard cash, and you are mine. Do you understand?"

The four intelligent topaz eyes stared back at her; they neither agreed nor disagreed.

"We are going to leave now," said Mrs. Muesli. "I came to this sale room on foot. But I am going to ride away in style."

She lit the torches of the Fire Dogs, and climbed into the claret and green brougham, which was parked outside, guarded by a traffic warden.

"All right, are you, ma'am?" he asked, for he thought Hetty looked strangely pale. "Know how to drive that there contraption?"

"Yes, thank you, my man," she said, and tipped him a halfpenny.

"*Now!*" she said to the Fire Dogs, and she was thinking of her hard childhood, of the years of drudgery as a maid, doing other people's cleaning, of the years passed at Esclairmonde College learning spiteful spells, of the slow years spent in weaving a rope out of cobwebs and her own gray hair. "Now," she said to the Fire Dogs, "I want you to catch up all that wasted time for me again. I want you to take me back into the Past. I want to be young once more."

Obediently, the Fire Dogs started away, but now they did not run at their usual sober pace. No, they went like wild creatures who have just been released from three thousand years in prison; they went faster than light or sound, faster than thought or fear. And the electric carriage flew after them at an equal pace.

But before very long at this unbelievably fast speed, Hetty Sark was hurled out of her seat, just as the old sisters had been. She flew through the air like a bullet, and when she landed, it was not in the street; no, she found herself at the door of the bank, walking toward the strong room with the Duchess's note clutched in her hot hand. She was young again, and poor again, and frozen with terror. She gave her note into the guard's hand, while he nodded politely.

But then he gave the note a second look, his face changed, and he gestured to a higher official, who pressed a concealed button under a desk. Hetty, glancing about her like a trapped rat, saw that several men, some of them in uniform, were approaching her. . . .

Meanwhile the Fire Dogs went flashing on, farther and farther into the past, deeper and deeper, darker and darker, past the Bronze Age and the Iron Age and the Stone Age, past Rome, Alexandria, and Troy, until they themselves were no more than tiny puppies, apple-sized bundles of fur, until at last they found their happy, scrambling way back up the long flight of black basalt steps leading up to the throne of Solomon, the High King.

People in Thornwick began calling the copper beech Miss Wilhelmina, and the silver birch Miss Roberta. Nobody asked what had become of Mrs. Muesli. And as for the Fire Dogs, they were soon forgotten; indeed, quite quickly, people began to believe that they had never existed at all.

Potter's Gray

They were hurrying through the cold, windy streets of Paris to the Louvre Museum—young Grig Rainborrow, and the au pair girl, Anna. They visited the Louvre two or three times every week. Grig would far rather have gone to one of the parks, or walked along by the river, but Anna had an arrangement to meet her boyfriend, Eugène, in the Louvre; so that was where they went.

Alongside one of the big main galleries, where hung huge pictures of battles and shipwrecks and coronations, there ran a linked series of much smaller rooms containing smaller pictures. Here visitors seldom troubled to go; often the little, rather dark rooms would be empty and quiet for a half hour at a time. Anna and Eugène liked to sit side by side, holding hands, on a couple of stiff upright metal chairs, while Grig had leave to roam at will through the nest of little rooms; though Anna tended to get fidgety if he wandered too far away, and would call him back in a cross voice, "Grig! Grig, where are you?

228

Where have you got to? Come back here now!" She worried about kidnapers, because of the importance of Grig's father, Sir Mark. Grig would then trail back reluctantly, and Eugène would grin at him, a wide, unkind grin, and say, "*Venez vite, petit mouton!*" Grig did not like being called a sheep, and he detested Eugène, who had large untrustworthy mocking black eyes, like olives; they were set so far apart in his face that they seemed able to see around the back of his head. He had a wide, oddly shaped mouth; his curling lips were thick and strongly curved like the crusts of farmhouse bread, and his mouth was always twisting about; it never kept still. Grig had once made some drawings of Eugène's mouth, but they looked so nasty that he tore them up before Anna could see them; he thought they might make her angry.

"Hurry up!" said Anna, jerking at Grig's hand. "We're going to be late. Eugène will be waiting; he'll be annoyed." Grig did not see why it would hurt Eugène to wait a few minutes, he never seemed to have anything to do but meet Anna in the Louvre museum. That was where they had met in the first place.

Standing waiting to cross the Rue de Rivoli at a traffic light, Grig was sorry that he lacked the courage to say, "Why do we have to meet hateful Eugène almost every day?"

But he knew that his courage was not up to that. Anna could be quite fierce. She had intense blue eyes the color of marbles, but they weren't very good for observing. Grig noticed a million more things than Anna did, he was

229

always saying, "Look, Anna—" And she would say, "Oh, never mind that! Come along!" But the stare of her eyes was so piercing when she lost her temper, they were like two gimlets boring right through him, and she had such a way of hissing, "You *stupid* child!" making him feel pulpy, breathless, and flattened, that he did not say what he felt about Eugène. He kept quiet and waited for the lights to change, while French traffic poured furiously past in a torrent of steel, rubber, and glass.

"Come on! There's a gap—we can go," said Anna, and jerked at Grig's hand again.

They hurled themselves out, in company with a French girl who had a small child in a stroller and, bounding on the end of his lead, a large Alsatian dog that the girl could only just control. As they crossed, the stroller veered one way, the dog tugged the other—it seemed amazing that the trio had survived among the traffic up to this day. A tall thin white-haired man in pink-tinted glasses observed their plight, and turned to give the girl a helping hand with her wayward stroller; a sharp gust of wind blew just at that moment, the dog tugged, the stroller swerved crazily, and the pink-tinted glasses were jerked off the man's face to spin away into the middle of the road, just as a new wave of traffic surged forward.

With a cry of anguish, the white-haired man tilted the stroller over the curb, hurriedly passing its handle into the mother's grasp, and then turned back to retrieve his glasses. Too late—and a terrible mistake: a motorcyclist, twisting aside to avoid him, collided with a taxi, and a

Citroën following too close behind the cycle struck the elderly man on the shoulder and flung him onto the sidewalk, where he lay on his face without moving.

If he had been wearing his glasses at that moment, they would have been smashed, Grig thought.

The mother with the stroller let out a horrified wail, *"Oh, oh, c'est le vieux Professeur Bercy!"* and she ran to kneel by him, while, out in the road, all was confusion, with brakes squawking and horns braying, and a general tangle and snarl of traffic coming too suddenly to a stop.

Police, blowing their whistles, were on the spot in no time—there are always plenty of police near the Louvre.

"Come along, Grig!" snapped Anna. "We don't want to get mixed up in all this, your father wouldn't be a bit pleased—" for Sir Mark, Grig's father, was the British Ambassador in Paris. But it wasn't easy to get away; already the police were swarming around, asking everybody there if they had seen the accident.

"Oh, I do *hope* the poor man is not badly hurt!" cried the distraught young mother. "It is Professor Bercy, the physicist—I have often seen his face in the papers and on TV—It was so kind of him to take my baby carriage— oh, it will be terrible if he is badly injured, and all because he stopped to help me—"

A gendarme was talking to Anna, and, while she snappishly but accurately gave an account of what had happened, Grig slipped out into the street and picked up the professor's glasses, which he had noticed lying—astonishingly, quite unharmed—about six feet out from the edge of the road, among a glittering sprinkle of some-body's smashed windshield.

"*Grig! Will* you come out of there!" yelled Anna, turn-ing from the cop to see where he had got to, and she yanked his arm and hustled him away in the direction of the Louvre entrance, across the big quadrangle, before he could do anything about giving the pink-tinted glasses to one of the policemen.

"But I've got these—"

"Oh, who cares? The man's probably dead, he won't want them again. If he hears that you got mixed up in a street accident your father will be hopping mad. And Eugène will be upset—he'll be wondering where we've got to."

It seemed to Grig that the last of these three statements was the real reason why Anna didn't want to hang around at the scene of the accident. He pulled back from her grasp and twisted his head round to see if an ambulance had arrived yet; yes, there it went, shooting across the end of the square with flashing lights. So at least the poor man would soon be in the hospital.

Well, it was true that if he was unconscious—and he had looked dreadfully limp—he wouldn't be needing his glasses right away.

Maybe he only wore them outdoors.

I'll ask mother to see that he gets them, Grig decided. She'll be able to find out which hospital he has gone to, and make sure that the glasses are taken to him. Mother was fine at things like that; she always knew what must be done, and who was the best person to do it. She understood what was important. And—Grig thought— the glasses must be *very* important to Professor Bercy, or he would hardly have risked his life in the traffic to try to recover them. Could they be his only pair? Surely not. If he was such an important scientist, you'd think he'd have dozens of pairs!

The glasses were now in Grig's jacket pocket, safely cradled in his left hand; the right hand was still in the iron grip of Anna, who was hauling him along as if the Deluge had begun and they were the last two passengers for the Ark.

Eugène was there before them, waiting in the usual room; but, surprisingly, he didn't seem annoyed at their lateness, just listened to Anna's breathless explanation with his wide frog-smile, said it was quite a little excitement they'd had, and did the man bleed a lot? Then, even more surprisingly, he produced a small patissier's cardboard carton, tied with shiny string, and said to Grig,

"Here, *mon mouton*, this is for you. For your *petit manger*. A cake."

Grig generally brought an apple to the Louvre. Indeed, he had one today, in his right-hand pocket. Eugène called the apple Grig's *petit manger*—his little snack. While Anna and Eugène sat and talked, Grig was in the habit of eating his apple slowly and inconspicuously, as he walked around looking at the pictures.

"Go on," repeated Eugène. "The cake's for you."

Grig did not want to appear rude or doubtful or

suspicious at this unexpected gift; but just the same he *was* suspicious. Eugène had never before showed any friendly feelings; the things he said to Grig were generally sharp or spiteful or teasing; why, today, should he have brought this piece of patisserie—rather expensive it looked, too, done up so carefully with a gold name on the side of the box. Eugène was always shabby, in worn jeans and a rubbed black-leather jacket, and his sneakers looked as if they let in the water. Why should he suddenly bring out such an offering?

"Say thank you!" snapped Anna. "It's very kind of Eugène to have brought you a cake!"

"Thank you," said Grig. He added doubtfully, "But I don't think people are allowed to eat in here."

"Oh, don't be silly. Who's going to see? Anyway, you always eat your apple—here, I'll undo the string."

It was tied in a hopelessly tight, hard knot—Anna nibbled through it with her strong white teeth, and Eugène made some low-voiced remark, in French too quick for Grig to catch, which made her flush and laugh, though she looked rather cross. Once the string was undone, the little waxed box opened out like a lily to disclose a gooey glistening brown cake in a fluted paper cup.

"Aren't you lucky; it's a rum baba," said Anna.

As it happened, a rum baba was Grig's least favorite kind of cake: too syrupy, too squashy, too scented. He wasn't greatly surprised, or disappointed; he would have expected Eugène to have a nasty taste in cakes, or anything else. He thanked Eugène again, with great politeness, then strolled away from the pair at a slow, casual pace, looking at the pictures on the walls as he went.

"Eat that up fast, now, or it'll drip syrup all over everywhere," Anna called after him sharply, and then she began talking to Eugène, telling him some long story, gabbling it out, while he listened without seeming to take in much of what she said, his eyes roving after Grig, who wandered gently into the next room, and then into the one after that, wondering, as he went, if it would be possible to slip the pastry into a litter bin without being noticed.

"Don't go too far now—" he could hear Anna's voice, fainter in the distance behind him.

As usual, there weren't any other people in the suite of small dark rooms. Grig supposed that the pictures here were not thought to be very important, though some of them were his particular favorites.

There was one of an astronomer with a globe; Grig always liked to look at that; and another of a woman making lace on a pillow; she wore a yellow dress, and had a contented, absorbed expression that reminded Grig of his mother while she was working on her embroidery. There was a picture that he liked of a bowl and a silver mug, with some apples; and another of a china jug with bunches of grapes and a cut-up pomegranate that he deeply admired. Grig intended to be a painter himself by and by; he always stood before this picture for a long, long time, wondering how many years it took to learn to paint like that—so that you could actually see the bloom on the grapes and the shine on the pearl handle of the knife, and the glisten on the red seeds of the pomegranate. Then there was a picture of a boy about Grig's age, sitting at a desk, playing with a spinning top. The boy was really a bit old to be playing with a childish toy such as a top; you could see that he had just come across it, maybe among some forgotten things at the back of his desk, and had taken it out to give it a spin because he was bored and had nothing better to do just then; he was watching it thoughtfully, consideringly, in fact he had the same intent expression as that on the face of the woman working at the lace on her pillow. Perhaps, thought Grig, that boy grew up to be some kind of scientist or mathematician (he must have lived long ago, for he wore an old-fashioned satin jacket) and at the sight of the spinning top, some interesting idea about speed or circles or patterns or time had come into his head. The boy with the top was one of Grig's favorite pictures, and he always stood in front of it for quite a while.

Then he was about to move on to his very favorite of all, when his attention was caught by an old lady, who had been walking through the rooms in the contrary direction. She paused beside Grig and glanced out through the window into the big central courtyard. What she saw there seemed to surprise her very much and arouse her disapproval too. She let out several exclamations—"*Oh, la la! Tiens! Quel horreur!*"—put on a pair of long-distance glasses to take a better look at what was going on outside, stared frowningly for a moment or two more,

236

then muttered some grumbling comment to herself, in which Grig caught several references to Napoleon III; then, shaking her head in a condemning manner, she went stomping on her way. After waiting until she was out of sight, Grig put a knee on the leather window seat and hoisted himself up to look out, in order to see what was happening outside that aroused such feelings of outrage in the old girl.

What he saw in the quadrangle made him surprised that he had not noticed it as they made their way in; but he remembered that then he had been looking back for the ambulance, and worrying about Professor Bercy's glasses; that must have been why he did not take in the oddness of the scene.

A wooden barricade had been built around the central part of the quadrangle, and it seemed that digging was going on inside this fence, a big excavator with its grabbing jaw could be seen swinging its head back and forth, dumping soil and rubble in a truck that stood by the paling.

Then, outside the barrier—and this was probably what had shocked the old lady—three fullsize chestnut trees lay, crated up, on huge towing trucks, the sort that usually carry heavy machinery, or sardinelike batches of new cars. The trees all had their leaves on, and their roots too; the roots had been carefully bundled up in great cylindrical containers made from wooden slats—like flower tubs, only a million times bigger, Grig thought. It appeared that the trees had been dug up from the central area and were being taken away, perhaps to be replanted somewhere else, just like geraniums or begonias in the public gardens. What on earth could Napoleon III have to do with it? Grig wondered, thinking of the old lady. Had he planted the trees, perhaps? They looked as if they could easily be over a hundred years old. Napoleon III had done a lot to beautify Paris, Grig knew. Perhaps among the roots of the trees, now parceled up like bean sprouts, there might be coins, francs and centimes from 1850, or medals or jewels, or all kinds of other relics. I'd love to have a closer look at them, thought Grig, and his left hand happened to touch Professor Bercy's sunglasses in his jacket pocket at the moment this thought came to him; he absentmindedly pulled out the glasses and perched them on his nose.

They fitted him quite well. He could feel that the earpieces were made out of some light, strong, springy material that clung, of its own accord, not uncomfortably, to the sides of his head. The lenses, squarish in shape, were very large; in fact they almost entirely covered his face, so that he could see nothing except through their slightly pinkish screen. For a moment they misted over, after he had put them on; then they began to clear, and he looked through them, out of the window and into the courtyard.

For years and years and years afterward, Grig went over and over that scene in his memory, trying to recall every last detail of it. When he had grown up, and become a painter, he painted it many times—the whole scene, or bits of it, small fragments, different figures from it—over and over and over again. "Ah, that's a Rainborrow," people would say, walking into a gallery, from thirty, forty feet away, "You can always tell a Rainborrow."

What did he see? He would have found it almost impossible to give a description in words. "*Layers,*" he thought. "It's like seeing all the layers together. Different levels. People now—and people *then*. People when? People right on back to the beginning. How many thousands of years people must have been doing things on this bit of ground! And, there they all are!"

As well as the people *then*, he could see the people *now*; several students, a boy riding a bicycle, a policeman, and the three great chestnut trees, tied on their trucks like invalids on stretchers. And, sure enough, in among the roots of the trees, Grig could catch a glimpse of all kinds of objects, knobby and dusty, solid and sparkling; perhaps that was what Professor Bercy had been coming to look at? The glasses must have had a fairly strong magnifying power, as well as this other mysterious ability they had, to show the layers of time lying one behind another.

What else could they show?

Grig turned, carefully, for he felt a little dizzy, to look inward at the room behind him. The first thing that caught his gaze, as he turned, was Eugène's gift, the rum baba, which he still clutched awkwardly in his right hand. Through Professor Bercy's pink-tinted glasses the cake looked even nastier than it had when seen by the naked eye. It was darker in color—the dark blood-brown, oozy and horrible; embedded in the middle of it he now saw two pills, one pink, one yellow. The pills hadn't been visible before, but through the pink lenses Grig could see them quite distinctly; sunk in the wet mass of dough they were becoming a bit mushy at the edges, beginning to wilt into the surrounding cake.

Why should Eugène want to give him cake with pills in it? What in the world was he up to? With a jerk of disgust, Grig dropped the little patisserie box on the floor. Nobody else was in the room. With his heel, he slid box and cake out of view under the window seat, then wiped his fingers—the syrup had already started to ooze through the carton—wiped his fingers vigorously, again and again, on a tissue. He glanced behind him to make sure that his action had not been seen by Anna or Eugène—but no, thank goodness, they were still safely out of sight, several rooms away.

Turning in the opposite direction, Grig walked quickly into the next room, where his favorite picture of all hung.

This was a painting of a horse, by an artist called Potter. Grig always thought of it as Potter's Gray. The picture was not at all large: perhaps one foot by eighteen inches, if as much; and the horse was not particularly handsome, rather the contrary. It was a gray, with some blobby dark dappled spots. Grig could hardly have said why he liked it so much. He was sure that the painter must have been very fond of the horse. Perhaps it belonged to him. Perhaps he called it Gray, and always gave it an apple or a carrot before sitting down with his easel and his tubes or pots of paint. The picture was over three hundred years old; a label said that Potter had been a Dutchman who lived from 1625 to 1654. He was only twenty-nine when he died, not old. Mother, who knew all sorts of things, once told Grig that Potter died of tuberculosis, which could have been cured these days. Grig thought that very sad. If Potter had lived now, he could have painted many more pictures of horses, instead of having his life cut off in the middle..

Anyway, this Gray was as good a horse as you could wish to meet, and, on each visit to the Louvre, Grig always walked to where his portrait hung, on the left of the doorway, between door and window, and—after first checking to make certain no one else was in the room— stood staring until his whole mind was filled with pleasure, with the whole essence of the horse; then he would pull the apple out of his pocket, take a bite of it himself, hold the rest up on the palm of his hand as you should when feeding a horse, and say, "Have a bite, Gray."

He did so now. But this time, something happened that had never happened before.

Gray put a gentle, silvery muzzle with soft nostrils sprouting white hairs out of the picture *and took the apple from Grig's hand.*

Then he withdrew his head into the frame and ate the apple with evident satisfaction.

Grig gasped. He couldn't help it—he was so pleased that he felt warm tears spring into his eyes. Blinking them away, he looked rapidly around the small gallery—and saw, without any particular surprise, that every picture was alive, living its life in its own way as it must have done when the artist painted it: a fly was buzzing over the grapes that lay beside the china jug, some men were hauling down the sail of a ship, the woman, winding the bobbins of her lace pillow, carefully finished off one and began another. Then she looked up and gave Grig an absent-minded smile.

There were other people in the room too, outside the pictures, walking about—people in all kinds of different clothes. Grig wished, from the bottom of his heart, that he could hear what they were saying, wished he could speak to them and ask questions—but Professor Bercy's glasses were only for seeing, they couldn't help him to hear. You'd want headphones too, Grig thought, straining his ears nonetheless to try and catch the swish of a dress, the crunch of Gray finishing the apple—but all he heard was the angry note of Anna's voice, "*Grig!* Where in the *world* have you *got* to?" and the clack of her wooden-soled shoes on the polished gallery floor as she came hurrying in search of him. Grig couldn't resist glancing back at Potter's horse—but the apple was all finished, not a sign of it remained—then he felt Anna's fingers close on his wrist like pincers, and she was hurrying him toward the exit, angrily gabbling into his ear. "What in heaven's name have you been *doing* with yourself all this time? Can't you see it's started to rain and we'll be late, we'll have to take a taxi—"

All this time she was hurrying Grig through one gallery after another, and Eugène was walking beside them, looking a little amused, and calmly indifferent to Anna's scolding of her charge.

Grig himself was still dizzy, shaken, confused, and distracted. Firstly, he would have liked to stop and stare with minute attention at each of the huge canvases they were now passing in the main galleries. Because—just *look* at what was happening in that coronation scene with Emperor Napoleon putting the crown on his queen's head, and the Pope behind him—and those people struggling to keep on the raft which was heaving about among huge waves—but some of them were dead, you could see—and the lady lying twiddling her fingers on a sofa— and the man on a horse—they were all alive, it was like looking through a series of windows at what was going on beyond the glass.

But also, Grig was absolutely horrified at what he saw when he looked across Anna at Eugène; the sight of Eugène's face was so extremely frightening that Grig's eyes instantly flicked away from it each time; but then he felt compelled to look back in order to convince himself of what he had seen.

All the *workings* were visible: inside the skull the brain— inside the brain, memory, feelings, hopes and plans. The memories were all dreadful ones, the hopes and plans were all wicked. It was like, from the height of a satellite, watching a great storm rage across a whole continent; you could see the whirl of cloud, the flash of lightning; you could guess at uprooted trees, flooded rivers, and smashed buildings. You could see that Eugène planned to do an enormous amount of damage; and it was plain that, here and now, he hated Grig and had a plan about him; what kind of a plan Grig didn't exactly know, but little details of it that came to him in flashes made him shudder.

"Come on, hurry up," said Anna, buttoning her raincoat, when they reached the entrance lobby. "Button your jacket, put your scarf around. Eugène's getting a taxi, and he'll drop us at the embassy and go on—"

"No!" said Grig. He didn't intend going with Eugène in any taxi. And he knew well that Eugène had no plans at all to drop them at the embassy.

"What do you mean, no?" said Anna furiously. "What in the world are you talking about? Don't act like a baby. You'll do as I say, or else—"

"No," repeated Grig doggedly, and yanked at the wrist which she still grasped in an unshakable grip. He looked at Anna and saw that she was not wicked like Eugène, but stupid all through, solid like a block of marble or plaster. It would be useless to argue with her and say, "Eugène is bad. He has some awful plan. Why did he put pills in that cake?"

Grig was still terribly confused and distracted by the complicated sights, the layers and layers of different happenings that were taking place all around him. But at last he realized what he must do. With his free hand he pulled the pink-tinted glasses off his face, and said, "Please, Anna. Put these on for a moment."

"Oh, don't be so *silly!* Why in the world should I? Where ever did you *get* those glasses?" She had forgotten all about the accident, and Professor Bercy. "What is this, anyway, some kind of silly joke?"

"Please put them on, Anna. If you don't—" What could he do, what could he possibly do? Then, with a gulp of relief, he remembered some practical advice that his mother had once given him. "It sounds babyish," she had said, "but if ever you are in a tight corner, *yell.* It attracts attention; people will come running, and that will give you time to think, so never mind that you may feel a fool, just do it, just yell."

"If you don't put them on," said Grig, "I shall scream so loud that people will think I've gone mad. I mean it, Anna."

"I think you already *have* gone mad," she said, but she looked at him, saw that he did mean it, and put on the glasses. At that moment Eugène came back through the glass entrance door, his black leather jacket shiny with rain, and on his face a big false smile. Without the glasses, Grig could no longer see the evil workings of Eugène's brain—which was in every way a relief—but just the same, he knew exactly how false that smile was.

"Okay," said Eugène, *"venez vite, tous les deux—"* and then Anna, looking at him, started to scream. Her scream was far, far louder than any yell that Grig could have raised, he had no need even to open his mouth. The smile dropped from Eugène's face like paper off a wet window, he stared at Anna first with shock, then with rage. "*Come* on, girl, what *is* this?" he said, trying to grab her hand, but she twisted away from him, still shrieking like a machine that has blown off its safety valve. "No— no—no—get away—get away—you're *horrible*—"

By this time, as Mother had prophesied, people were running toward them; people were staring and exclaiming and pushing close, trying to discover what was the matter with Anna. Now Eugène's nerve suddenly broke. He let out a couple of wicked, hissing swearwords, turned on his heel, went out the glass doors, and vanished from view. At the same moment Anna, furiously dragging the tinted glasses from her face, flung them on the stone floor as if they were poisoned, trampled them into fragments, and burst into hysterical sobs.

"Would you please telephone my father?" Grig said to a uniformed woman who seemed like someone in a position of authority. "I think my *gouvernante* has been taken ill. My father is the British Ambassador," and he gave her the embassy number.

So they went home in a taxi after all.

"Please, can you take me to see Professor Bercy in the hospital?" Grig asked his mother, the next day, when Anna was under sedatives and the care of a doctor, and a new au pair girl was being advertised for, and in the meantime Lady Julia Rainborrow was leaving her ambassadorial duties to take her son for an airing.

But she said, "Darling, no; I'm afraid I can't. It was

on the news this morning. He died last night in the hospital; he never recovered consciousness."

"Oh," said Grig. "Oh."

He had dreaded having to tell Professor Bercy that his glasses had been smashed; but this was far worse.

I wonder if they *were* his only pair? Grig thought, plodding along the street beside Lady Julia. Or if other people—the other scientists who worked with him—knew about them too?

"Where would you like to go?" Grig's mother asked him. "It's not a very nice day—I'm afraid it looks like rain again."

"Can we go to the Louvre?"

"Are you sure you want to go there?" she said doubtfully.

"Yes, I would like to," said Grig, and so they walked in the direction of the Louvre, finding it hard to talk to each other, Grig very unhappy about Professor Bercy, dead before he had finished his life's work—and what work!—while Lady Julia worried about Grig. But what can you do? You can't look after somebody twenty-four hours a day. Ambassadors' sons have to take their chances, like everybody else.

Going quickly through the suite of dark little galleries, Grig came to the picture of Potter's Gray. He stood and stared at the dappled horse, very lovingly, very intently, and thought: Yesterday I gave you an apple, and you put out your head and took it from my hand, and I stroked

247

your nose. I shall come back tomorrow, and next week, and the week after, and that will never, never happen again. But it *did* happen, and I remember it.

Do you remember it, Gray?

He thought that the gray horse looked at him very kindly.